QUIET AS THE GRAVE

ERIK CARTER

AUTHOR NOTE

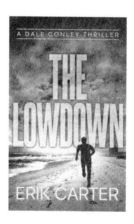

IF YOU ENJOY the book you're about to read and would like different take on the same core story, check out my novel, *The Lowdown*, an action thriller in my other series.

I adapted *The Lowdown* as the basis for *Quiet as the Grave*, so as an introduction to my other series—the Dale Conley series—you might enjoy seeing a different take on the story and checking out the similarities and differences between *The Lowdown* and *Quiet as the Grave*.

If you enjoy the Silence Jones series, I'm certain you'll love the Dale Conley series as well. It's set in the groovy '70s and features a headstrong, cocky, yet competent hero who travels the country solving history-related crimes.

CHAPTER ONE

Reno, Nevada
The 1990s

PEOPLE WERE EXPENDABLE. Especially worthless ones like the person a few yards away, leaning against the wall, drooling on himself, giggling like a fool.

There were close to five and a half billion humans in the world. Projections showed that by the end of the 1990s, humanity would hit six billion. A decade into the new millennium, there would be seven billion. By the year 2025, there would be over eight billion.

Brooks Garrity was born in the early '70s. Then, there had been less than four billion. That meant the world's population will have *doubled* in his lifetime, before he even reached the age of sixty.

So Brooks had no qualms about thinning the herd a little. Hell, he *wasn't* thinning the herd. There was nothing a single man could do against the relentless spread. Brooks's work was a proverbial drop in the ocean. Which meant it was harmless.

He crossed through the area between the two buildings,

which wasn't so much an alley as it was a gap—just a dark, cramped space a few yards long. It would have been an all-but-forgotten bit of nothingness were it not positioned just a few short blocks from Reno's main hustle and bustle.

It wasn't completely silent—was there anywhere in Reno, this miniature Las Vegas, that was entirely quiet at nighttime? —but the *ring-a-ding-ding* sounds of slot machines and the digital fanfare of electronic poker along with the laughter and murmur of traffic playing off the brick walls were softened by distance. Everything sounded echoey, almost surreal.

Louder than the distance-muffled debauchery was the giggling of the young man in front of Brooks. The guy's back was planted against the wall, legs at a sharp angle in front of him, barely keeping him vertical, arms dangling lifelessly. Brooks saw a drop of blood on the inside of his elbow where the kid had recently shot up. There were also track marks, indicators of other recent adventures—dark veins and a couple of pus-filled abscesses.

The guy was in his late teens, maybe early twenties. White. Lean. Brown hair in a buzz cut. Flannel button-up worn open over a T-shirt. Scraggly facial hair. A touch of light from a dying fixture on the wall a couple of yards above illuminated him. His head lulled side to side, and he murmured in between his bouts of giggling. But aside from Brooks, there was no one else around. The guy was talking to himself.

Just a worthless junkie, someone who'd thrown his life away before it even started.

Yes, Brooks was doing the world a favor.

Focus. Brooks needed to prepare. He could feel the muscles of his face tensed in a scowl, but to win the guy's attention—even in an inebriated state—Brooks would have to act friendly. He softened his features, trying to create a look that signaled innocence, even openness. The corners of his mouth turned upwards, and he widened his eyes slightly.

This was a talent of his—affecting the minute changes in appearance that convinced others, without saying a word, of one's demeanor, one's character. Brooks was a man brimming with character, with ideals, and he could manipulate that sincerity to his will. And people completely bought the act. Always. That's how Brooks had been able to achieve so much.

In his pocket was the weapon, another in a growing list of random knives. This one was a steak knife. Nondescript. Battered wooden handle. Scuffed-up blade. It even had a bit of rust. Brooks had bought it at a flea market that afternoon, pulled it out of a collection of random kitchenware that had been piled carelessly in a cracked plastic storage tub. Ten cents, it had cost him.

Ten cents for this much fun.

There were still a few cheap thrills left in the world.

He had improvised a sheath out of cardboard—just a small strip that he'd bent in half and stapled along one side. He'd left the blade plenty of breathing room so he could quickly yank it out.

As he wrapped his fingers around the wooden handle, he moved his lips a bit more, getting everything into place—a few final adjustments to an insincere visage. He continued toward the younger man.

A faint melody of music drifted across the distance, accompanying the cacophony of Reno's downtown casinos—laughter, traffic, drunkenness. An occasional shout or cheer or revving engine punctuated the din.

Reno. What a depraved place. Gambling. Debauchery. Indecency. "The Biggest Little City in the World" it was called. This sounded cutesy; it made Reno seem like something you wanted to scoop up with both hands and give a big warm hug to. Really, though, Reno was just a scaled-down version of its big brother, Las Vegas. A filthy place with filthy people, both the locals and the ones who chose to visit.

But Brooks's current location was separated from the glitz of the city center. He was in a different part of the city, relatively close to all the hubbub, but far enough away that there was some sense of normalcy.

It was less glitzy.

But more dangerous.

Brooks was willing to accept the danger for what he needed to do. This would be his fourth kill.

No, that wasn't entirely accurate.

He'd killed several, but he'd only knifed three. The man in front of him would be his fourth *immediate* kill, but there had been several others who'd died some time after Brooks had visited them.

He took the syringe from his pocket. This item was Brooks's original objective for the evening—another random distribution. It was to be his latest indirect kill.

Were he to use the syringe—as planned, as he'd been told to—and not the knife, death wouldn't happen there in the quasi-alley. It would happen days later, in a pissing, moaning pile on the man's bathroom floor. Or maybe he would collapse at work—that is, if the loser even had a job—eliciting shrieking terror from his coworkers.

In fact, were Brooks to give the man the syringe, the guy might not die at all. He might survive the syringe's contents and end up with permanently damaged insides. It had happened before.

After taking a good, hard look at the man, however, Brooks had decided against the tainted syringe and opted for his knife, that ten-cent beauty he'd purchased earlier in the day. He was just itching to cover it with hot blood. The knife attacks weren't in the initial plan, and soon enough, Ian Dalton would find out that Brooks had committed another stabbing. Dalton would be pissed.

But it was worth it.

Brooks checked the doorways as he walked, looking for vagrants or lost gamblers or burn-the-midnight-oil workers—anyone who might see what was about to happen. He found no one.

Perfect.

As he drew closer, the young man pulled his head up and brought a pair of glassed-over eyes in Brooks's direction.

"Join the party," the guy said and immediately guffawed, bending at the waist.

It was a deep laugh. A damned laugh. The laugh of someone in a Reno, Nevada, alley pissing his life away before it even began.

Brooks stepped up beside him, a few feet away. He fought the feelings of revulsion coursing through him. "Sorry to bother you. I need a little help."

The guy looked at him, blinked. Dilated pupils. Teetering, wobbling face.

"You're not the Carver, are you?"

The guy laughed again, heartily.

"The Carver?"

"Not from around here, huh?" the man said. "Some dude's been going around town for the last three weeks. Serial killer, they say. He'll carve ya up. *Pow! Pow!*" He pantomimed two knife strikes with his exclamations. "No one can catch the guy. Smart dude, I guess."

Brooks gave a polite chuckle.

"You're right. I'm not from around here, and I'm a little lost," he said, affecting a voice that matched the trust-worthy look on his face. "I'm staying at the Voyager Casino."

"The Voyager!" the younger man said and laughed louder. He scratched at the vile markings on the inside of his elbow. "That's like *a mile* from here, dude. Downtown. With the other casinos. How the hell'd you end up here?"

"Gee, I don't know," Brooks said and looked at the ground, rubbing the back of his neck bashfully.

"All right, man," the guy said, his laughter now subsiding. The crown of his head dropped back against the brick wall with a soft thump, and it started to rock side to side like it had been when Brooks first approached. "I can get you back to where you belong. But what's in it for me?"

Brooks laughed inwardly, almost externally. He had to fight to keep the disingenuous smile on his lips from breaking out in dark laughter—because this young man was an even bigger slime than he'd thought. Not only was he a junkie, but he was an opportunist.

Yes, Brooks had zero guilt about what he was going to do.

"You'll really help me out?" Brooks said, bringing the tone of his voice to the heights of his feigned purity.

"Sure, man. If the price is right," the guy said with a smile.

"How about this?" Brooks said and pulled the knife from his pocket, displaying it. He leaned close and whispered, "I *am* the Carver."

In a flurry of motion, Brooks rammed the knife deep into the other man's stomach, repeatedly jabbing and twisting. The guy gasped for air, and his lips formed an anguished but silent scream. Blood gushed from the wounds, dripping onto the pavement below them.

A final shove of the knife, and the younger man's body collapsed in a limp heap. His eyes were wide open, and a pool of blood creeped out from beneath his torso.

Dead. Asleep in the throes of violence. The Carver had struck again.

But he wasn't done.

Brooks fell upon the man, going to a knee, and drove the blade into his back a few more times, each strike followed by a thud and a wet squelching noise. Blood splashed out.

Brooks stopped, exhaled. He stood and checked the surroundings again, just in case.

Clear.

As he caught his breath, he stared down at the body and smiled.

He took only a moment to admire his handiwork before he hooked the body under the armpits and started dragging it to his truck.

CHAPTER TWO

SILENCE JONES PUSHED through the door, its heavy wood-and-metal frame creaking.

The sound of raucous laughter abruptly died.

Greeting him, a wall of hostile glares and an eerie, oppressive quiet. Silence stepped inside. Every conversation had stopped, and all eyes in the bar followed him. Even the music that had been playing came to an abrupt halt.

It was like a Wild West movie, where an out-of-town stranger walks into a saloon, and the piano player suddenly stops playing while the crowd hushes and stares at the newcomer who strolls insides, spurs jingling.

It was a bold move, possibly stupid, barging into a biker bar that by all accounts catered to a close-knit group of locals. What made the move even bolder was Silence's outfit, a glaring discrepancy to the other men in the place. He wore a pair of gray trousers, black derbies with high-traction rubber soles, and a lightweight gray striped Hugo Boss shirt under a well-paired Hugo Boss sport coat.

The men staring at him bore leather jackets and soiled T-shirts. Leather pants. Long gray hair. Long white hair.

Mustaches. Beards. Fat, powerful arms. There were only two women in the place, and they were much like the men in dress and appearance.

The reek of body odor was so thick that it overpowered the cigarette smoke and the tang of stale beer.

Yes, strolling into a place like this at 9:35 on a Thursday night was a bold move indeed.

But Silence was tired of waiting. He'd been in Reno for three days, lurking in the shadows, and his investigation had stalled. Technically speaking, he wasn't in Reno at the moment. He was in Spanish Springs, a community within the Reno area, but outside the city proper.

Silence took a lot of his wisdom from the teachings of his deceased fiancée, C.C., and one of her keenest pieces of holistic knowledge had been the concept of taking action. Sometimes, to make things happen, you simply gotta take action.

And Silence was a man of action.

So here he was.

At a biker bar with a dozen pairs of eyes staring perplexed yet deadly daggers into him.

Aside from C.C.'s wisdom of yesteryear, she also spoke to him in the present, a voice in his head that visited him regularly, offering advice and thoughts, often in high-tension moments.

Moments like this.

She spoke to him now.

Love? she said.

Silence's internal voice replied, *Yes?*

Why are you doing this?

I wasn't getting anywhere. I needed to take action.

You're being impetuous, C.C. said. *This is dangerous.*

And?

A long pause. Then C.C. sighed and said, *Well, be safe, I*

guess.

She left.

The phantom version of C.C. was often as flummoxed by Silence's headstrong qualities as the real-life woman had been.

It was a low-droopy-ceiling sort of place. A neon sign in the corner displayed the bar's name: *DESERT ROSE*. The walls bore motorcycle memorabilia, interspersed with a few dusty photographs. Neon lights tossed different colors into the gloom: red, blue, yellow. Three pool tables. A bathroom in the back. A wall of booths. Several round wooden tables.

And a long bar to the side, behind which the bartender—a man with long white-gray hair and a matching beard—watched Silence with interest and a wary eye to the underside of the counter, where there was likely a baseball bat or a shotgun.

Silence stood tall and unyielding, surveying the space, studying the rough-looking bikers, measuring angles.

Everyone kept staring at him.

"I'm looking for three people," Silence said, addressing the whole of the bar, sweeping the space with his eyes. He swallowed.

He hadn't shouted, but he'd been loud, authoritative, booming, and this brought a shot of pain to his throat. Years earlier, an incident had nearly killed him, and he was left with a damaged larynx. His throat was a wall of permanent scar tissue, so speaking was torturous. Abbreviated sentences and frequent swallowing helped to ease the torment.

"First, the Carver," he said and swallowed again. "Second, anyone with info..." Another swallow. "About Toscani's tainted heroin." Another swallow. "Last, Donald Judkins."

There was a pause—then the whole bar exploded into laughter and jeers. Every greasy biker cackled with glee.

Every biker except one...

He was one of the youngest. His face was blanched, and

sweat beaded his forehead, despite the chill in the air. The man's leather jacket was adorned with an eagle patch, neon green. While the rest of the energy in Desert Rose was focused on Silence, this man's eyes looked left and right, anywhere but Silence, and he inched toward the exit.

The beefed-up Santa Claus of a bartender came out from behind the counter and started toward Silence, eyes locked on him. In his left hand was the baseball bat Silence had assumed was stowed beneath the bar. As he approached, the other bikers came with him, the entire crowd creeping toward Silence.

Silence sensed the gathering, crackling energy of an impending bar room brawl. He'd taken part in a few. He knew the signs.

The bartender eyed him suspiciously as he approached.

"I know the name Donald Judkins," he said in a nasally voice that mismatched his appearance. "That sumbitch has an outstanding tab—over two hundred dollars. A lot of folks around town want to get their hands on Judkins. But you stroll in here in them sissy-looking clothes asking about a serial killer and Reno's mob boss. Makes me think you ain't to be trusted. Makes me nervous." He narrowed his eyes. "Can I trust you, big fella?"

As he finished his question, he put a smile on his bearded face. Not genuine. Sinister. And as he reached out to put a seemingly friendly hand on Silence's shoulder, Silence saw movement in the man's other hand.

The one holding the bat.

Silence moved with blinding speed. His arm shot up, and with one swoop of his palm, he cleanly ripped the bartender's hand off his shoulder. A crunching sound echoed through the room as the bartender's hand collapsed under Silence's grip, all those metacarpals grinding together. Silence brought them right to the point of snapping.

And held them there.

Tears swelled in the bartender's eyes as he emitted a bloodcurdling scream.

He dropped the bat. It clattered on the grimy linoleum. A moment later, Silence released the big man, who immediately fell to a knee.

The other bikers jumped forward without hesitation, but Silence was one step ahead. He instantly braced his fists and met them head-on.

Another huge guy lunged forward and threw a punch. Silence ducked to the side, dodging the blow and countering with a swift punch of his own that landed squarely on the biker's jaw.

The man staggered back, stunned, and Silence followed through with two more precise punches—ribs first, then the solar plexus. The man howled louder than the bartender had.

A barrel chested guy with a necklace made of 1/4-inch steel chain came at him next with a wild haymaker. Silence juked left, diving under the punch, and came back with an uppercut to the man's jaw.

The crowd erupted in fury.

Two more were on him. Then a third. One of Silence's punches was stopped by a beefy hand that clamped down on his forearm. Someone else caught his jacket.

Silence pulled forward, regaining his footing. He'd lost track of the opponents, his fists moving in fast, relentless circles of defense, sending punishing blows. He battled his way through them, ignoring the stings of small cuts and bruises inflicted on him.

As he fought, he kept stealing quick glances at the suspicious man wearing the neon green eagle patch. The man hadn't joined the fray. He was watching everything, but he was still going for the door, trying not to be noticed by the others, who surely all knew him.

This was a man with pride—or at least a reputation—but something about what Silence had announced to the crowd had made him want to leave the bar immediately.

Not only did Silence need to free himself from the mob that wanted his blood, his life, but he needed to do so quickly, or he was going to lose Eagle Patch. And he couldn't do that. Because something about the man's reaction said he knew something.

Something important.

Silence threw another man to the floor, sending him flying back in to the bar stools, cracking his head, going limp. This freed Silence momentarily, and as he squared up to the remaining bikers, they exchanged looks of disbelief before quickly dispersing, bolting off.

Silence looked to the exit.

Eagle Patch had taken advantage of the opportunity and was fleeing with the others. He slipped into the night.

Silence sprinted across the bar, pushing through the bottleneck of bikers. Outside, the air was dry, cool, and the sky was pitch black. Desert Rose's parking lot was dimly lit by a few flickering lamp poles.

He skidded to a stop. Several of the bikers were mounting Harleys, big engines firing up, thundering off onto the quiet side street. But where was...

There!

He saw Eagle Patch running away, down an alley at the side of the building, stealing glances over his shoulder. Silence took off again at a full sprint.

He breathed heavily as he raced down the alleyway and around the corner, the heavy thuds of his steps echoing in the darkness. He rounded another corner.

And found nothing.

The man had vanished. No sign of him in the darkness.

Shit!

There had to have been a damn good reason Eagle Patch got skittish back at the bar. Everyone in Reno was talking about the city's pair of scandals—the Carver serial killer and the heroin deaths linked to criminal boss Demetrio Toscani —so Silence wagered that Eagle Patch was more freaked out about the third name Silence had shouted out to the bikers: Donald Judkins.

He heard footsteps echoing ahead.

Silence ran harder, pulling past a crumbling brick wall, his shoes slipping on the wet street. He was closing the gap—the footsteps ahead were louder, nearer. He willed his legs to go even faster, and they burned with each step.

As he locked onto the sound ahead and turned a corner, he caught sight of the man. Eagle Patch was running fast, his figure barely visible in the night. He looked over his shoulder, made eye contact with Silence. His mouth opened wide in shock.

With a last burst of energy, Silence sprinted forward, closing the gap. He was yards away. Then only feet away.

Then he lunged.

Whack!

The man fell to the ground with a thud, and Silence rolled past him. In his copious training years earlier, Silence had been taught how to redirect his energy, and he tucked into a roll that landed him back on his feet. He spun around, squaring to the other man on the pavement.

There was a *click*, and an out-the-front switch blade flashed into existence from Eagle Patch's hand right when Silence lunged downward at him. Silence angled to the side as he dropped, just as the man stabbed at him—going for his torso—and the knife soared past, missing by inches.

In a bit of improvised aikido/brute strength, Silence angled the man's outstretched arm beneath his and gave him a quick pulse, torquing the weapon loose. The man screamed.

His fingers splayed out in a fireworks pattern, and the knife clattered on the pavement.

Panicking now, Eagle Patch tried to scramble up, but Silence twisted the arm farther, pinning him down. This was a big dude, but Silence quickly managed to subdue him, gripping his arm tightly and pushing it up behind his back.

"Who are you?" Silence said, panting from the effort of the chase. He swallowed. "How do you know..." He swallowed. "Donald Judkins? Talk!"

It was a gamble—assuming that the man had panicked about Judkins and not the other two names Silence had said. But Silence was confident in his assumption, and his gamble paid off when the man said, "Okay! Okay, man. We, uh..." He gulped. "We used to hit the casinos. Poker. Me and Donnie."

He paused, his eyes flickering side to side over Silence's.

"He ain't a bad dude, man. I swear! Don't kill the guy. He's not a friend or anything, but ... I ain't a snitch, all right?"

"Where is he?" Silence said.

The man's lips moved, trying but failing to say anything. He really *wasn't* a snitch.

Silence slammed him onto the pavement.

"*Talk!*"

"Okay, man! Okay! He's ... he's at the Silver Moon. Room 212. He doesn't have a place right now. He's in a real bad fix."

Silence released his grip, and immediately Eagle Patch scrambled to his feet and ran off into the night.

Silence watched the man disappear, then he slowly stood and brushed the dirt off his clothes. A quick inspection revealed no fraying, no holes, no tears. Silence offered himself a satisfied nod. He chose clothing as durable as it was chic— the stylistically conscientious assassin.

His clothes were unmarred, perhaps, but he wasn't. He ran a pair of exploratory hands over his body, wincing again and again as he found sore spots on his ribs, his left thigh, his jaw.

But his seemingly headstrong decision to barge into Desert Rose had been worth the pain. He had an address. He had a lead.

He had a chance to find Donald Judkins.

CHAPTER THREE

Brooks stood at a patch of weeds and bare earth that constituted a lawn. A line of mountains towered in the distance, a stunning violet slash against the star-speckled sky, but the desperate trailer park before him negated Nature's splendor. A flickering, orange-hued sodium bulb on a pole several yards away offered little assistance to the glow of stars and the moon. The park was bathed in shadows.

He was on the outskirts of the Reno metropolitan area, and the trailer before him was among the worst in the park. It needed a little paint work and a lot of rust removal. Tan on top, white on bottom with red accents. An awning of corrugated polycarbonate shielded a small wooden porch, and an air conditioner jutted at an awkward, drooping angle from one of the windows.

Brooks stared at the trailer, waiting for Ian Dalton. Brooks knew why he'd been summoned here—Dalton must have gotten word of what had happened earlier in the evening. He must have known that Brooks had gone off script, that the Carver had claimed another victim.

That's why Brooks had been waiting so long. Almost five minutes now. Standing in the evening chill.

Some people erroneously assumed Reno's climate was just like that of its big brother, Las Vegas. Both cities were gambling towns. Both were in the state of Nevada. On the surface, it made sense.

But Reno was in *northern* Nevada, while Las Vegas was in the desert. Though the evenings would get a lot colder in the coming months, this was a particularly chilly September, and the temperature had dropped another few degrees since Brooks knifed the guy. It was about forty degrees, and Brooks wasn't wearing a jacket. He shivered.

That's why Dalton was making him wait outside. Dalton wanted him to suffer the anticipation, not just inwardly but physically. Brooks himself had a knack for theatrics, so he understood what Ian was trying to accomplish when he did things like this. This objective analysis made Dalton's theatrics seem more benign, but still Brooks couldn't separate himself entirely from his gut, emotional reaction.

The truth was, Brooks was anxious. About what Dalton was going to do with him.

The door opened. Halfway. Paused. Then it swung open entirely, and out walked Ian Dalton. To look at him, you'd never know how magnificent he was. By appearances, he was average. If there had been a listing for *middle-aged, blue-collar white male*, Dalton's photo would have been next to it. He stood about five-foot-nine. Brown hair being steadily overtaken by white, particularly on the sides. Stubble beard, all-white. Brown eyes. A few wrinkles befitting a man in his mid-fifties.

At a glance, you'd never guess this man was a failed genius, a man who should be in another existence, not here in Reno —were it not for cruel fate. Early on, though, Brooks had seen past Dalton's ho-hum exterior. He'd immediately detected the man's greatness. He'd felt it, like a pulsing emanation coming right off Dalton, like a glow, an aura.

That's why he'd gravitated to him. And Dalton hadn't disappointed. He was leading Brooks to a better life.

Dalton wore heavily soiled jeans and an equally soiled neon green T-shirt with the company logo, telephone number, and name—*GARCIA LANDSCAPING SERVICES*. Brooks hadn't worked that day, and since Dalton bore a perennial disregard for his own appearance, Brooks couldn't be sure if Dalton was wearing the shirt post-shift or if he'd simply worn the shirt on a day he wasn't working.

Dalton held a bottle of Bud in his hand. He blinked at Brooks, adjusting to the darkness. Waited for a moment. Then descended the stairs, taking a long swig. He maintained eye contact as he approached. He stopped a few feet from Brooks, looked him up and down. Laughed.

"You pathetic piece of shit." Dalton's words oozed contempt. He'd scoffed when he said it, and his eyes were nothing but pure malice. "So ... Brooks just had to stab another one, huh?"

"I ... I only ... you told me it was okay!" Brooks pleaded. "He was a nobody; I'm sure of it! No one's going to look for him, and—"

"I told you it was okay *if you were careful!*" Brooks's voice boomed, and he immediately looked to the next-door trailer, making sure his neighbor, Hal, hadn't heard. His eyes flicked back to Brooks. "Someone saw you, moron. The Carver legend grows because of your sloppiness."

Dalton took another long, vicious swig of his beer, staring into Brooks.

Brooks took a step back.

"I ... I thought I was careful." Brooks avoided Dalton's

eyes. He looked to the ground and back up. Found him staring still.

Ian spun the bottle in his hand as he assessed Brooks. "It's your fault I'm in this predicament, Brooks."

Brooks hated apologizing to people. He hated lowering himself like that. But he reminded himself again of his need to remain humble if he was going to be permitted to continue with his righteous quest.

"I'm sorry," he said.

Dalton scoffed. "I gave you an opportunity. The partners have sunk a fortune in this. My reputation, my *entire life,* is on the line. And you're out there taking chances with your sick indulgences."

He paused to stare silently at Brooks for a moment, then went for another swig, halted. Holding the bottle a few inches out, he saw that it was empty. He heaved it, and Brooks watched it fly out into the rocky wilderness beyond the trailer park, land, shatter.

He brought his attention back to Dalton.

"If you put this in jeopardy one more time," Dalton said, "I'll deal with you personally. I think you know what that means." A pause. "Have you found any more of the symbols?"

As soon as he finished the question, he turned toward the trailer. Brooks stayed where he was. Ian didn't want him to follow; he only wanted him to answer, there in his ordained spot of shame.

"I ... No. No, I didn't. Not tonight. I—"

Dalton stopped on the trailer's small front porch, pivoting, swinging his gaze back on Brooks. "No, you were too busy perforating a nobody."

Brooks couldn't bear the indignation anymore, couldn't take Dalton's dark stare. He looked down at the barren brown stone beneath his boots as he said, "I'm going to track down

Calypso. I can figure out where the symbols came from, Ian. I promise you."

Dalton scoffed. And in a dark tone that married up to his implied threat of moments earlier, he said, "You sure as hell better hope you do."

Brooks looked up and watched as Dalton stepped into the trailer. The screen door slapped shut behind him.

CHAPTER FOUR

ASIDE FROM A COUPLE of transitory stops at Reno-Tahoe International, Silence had never been to Reno, Nevada, despite years of cross-country and international travels.

Reno had a lot going for it. It was neither too big nor too small, hence its nickname, "The Biggest Little City in the World." Good weather. A close proximity to Lake Tahoe and other natural wonders. Cultural activities. Nightlife. And, of course, the casinos.

But there was normality in the city, too. Since becoming an assassin, Silence had spent most of his life traveling, and if one travels long enough, one discovers that cities with celebrated features also have massive regions of normality—just everyday, bland, humanity. Miles and miles of supermarkets, bus stops, shopping malls, highway cloverleafs, liquor stores.

He was currently in just such an area of Reno. This was not the glitzy downtown, with the multi-colored bright lights of the casino towers sparkling off the beloved Truckee River. No, this was simply real life—a rough, industrial region of town, just outside the city proper. And Silence was outside a rat's nest called the Silver Moon Motel, whose flickering sign indicated *HBO, SWIMMING POOL,* and *SLOT MACHINES.*

It was a big, two-story rectangle, white with faded blue around the trim and the front office. The doors were faded as well, a light coral color that must have been maroon at one time. A few of the windows were covered with particleboard. Weeds grew in the cracks of the parking lot, which was occupied by old, tired-looking vehicles. A few sad plants clung to the side of the building, toward the back. Silence heard desperate laughter, blaring televisions, a shouting match.

At the far end of the parking lot was a pair of battered dumpsters. Silence was beside them, knelt over, and next to him, sitting with his back against the fence, was a snakelike man—long and lean and slithery. A round head on a long neck. Thin in the way that only a drug addict could be, a theory that was confirmed by the bruising and angry pink dots on the inside of the man's left elbow.

Silence pointed at the man's self-imposed markings. "Toscani?"

The man giggled. "Hell, it's all Toscani's in Reno, brother. Best shit outside California."

Silence had known about Demetrio Toscani's stranglehold on Reno long before he'd arrived three days earlier, but it had taken several instances of firsthand exposure like this for him to fully realize the man's impact on the city.

On the crumbling blacktop beside the snake-man was a small hypodermic; the plunger's rubber stopper was pressed all the way down. Empty.

The flickering, orange-ish streetlight above caught something on the end of the barrel. A slight indentation.

Silence leaned farther down. Carefully, he pinched the syringe between two fingers, lifted it to the faint light.

There were markings on the end of the barrel. Hand-drawn, scratched into the plastic. A triangle, a circle, and a square.

Immediately, Silence recognized that they were some sort of labeling system, something Toscani's people had implemented to inventory their goods without leaving a trail for the Reno police.

As an assassin for the Watchers—a group of well-meaning but technically criminal individuals embedded within in the U.S. government with the mission of correcting injustices— Silence had received copious training in a wide variety of topics. One of the subjects had been cryptography; however, it was a field of study so varied, complex, mathematical, and esoteric that he understood that his knowledge only scratched the surface.

There was someone he knew—*used to* know, rather—who might be able to make sense of the symbols.

But his memories of that person were fractured.

And difficult.

He wouldn't worry about it now. Besides, he was in Reno for the serial killer, the Carver, not Toscani.

Refocusing, he placed the syringe back where it had come from, faced the man below him, and took the photo of Judkins from his back pocket. He held it a few inches in front of Snake's face.

He'd been showing it all over town. Lots of people recognize Donald Judkins. Few wanted to talk.

The image showed a forty-something white guy leaning over a roulette table. His brown hair was shaggy, sitting somewhere between avant-garde and out-of-style. He wore a sport coat and a button-up shirt, undone halfway down his chest. His expression was serious, and the bags under his eyes and the lines etching his face said that his days of taking joy from the casino experience were somewhere in the past.

"Know him?" Silence said.

The Snake looked up, studied the photo, laughed again and resumed rolling the crown of this head back and forth against the dumpster.

That was his only response.

Silence took a deep breath, repressed his frustration.

"Donald Judkins. Staying in..." he said and swallowed before pointing behind him to room 212 on the balcony above. "212. When last..." He swallowed. "See him?"

Using broken, shortened English was another of Silence's techniques to help with his tortured throat.

Snake opened his eyes, squinted at the photo, and that little grin dropped from his face.

"*That* dude?" he said, coming to life, crawling his backside up the dumpster. "Oh, shit. Oh, shit. I gotta go."

He slithered to his feet, and Silence stood up as well, grabbing Snake's wrist before he could dart off.

"Wait."

"No way, man. I'm out."

Snake tried to bolt, but didn't budge. This was a small man, and Silence's strength was legendary.

"Just want to talk," Silence said.

Snake might not have had any advantage over Silence physically, but this was the kind of guy who was a conniving survivalist, so he improvised with surprising acuity—by grabbing the empty hypodermic and stabbing it at Silence.

Of course, the needle itself posed no threat. Rather, it was the threat of the *disease* it very well might hold. A guy like Snake was likely ill with something, and he would know that a guy like Silence would recognize that fact.

Silence released his grasp on Snake's arm and stepped back, dodging the swing of the needle. He squared up, assessing the situation and readying himself for a fight.

The two men circled each other for a few moments before Snake made his next move. He lunged at Silence with the needle leading, thrusting like a fencer. Silence grabbed his arm, twisted it behind his back, forcing him to drop the syringe.

"Just want to talk," Silence said again.

He eased Snake back around and lessened his grip on the man's wrist. The guy had been minding his own business when he arrived and hadn't done anything to harm him.

...aside from the syringe attack.

So it was time for a bit of back-alley diplomacy.

"Where's Judkins?" Silence said.

"You'll let me go if I tell you?"

Silence nodded.

Snake bit his lip. "Okay, he left two days ago. I don't know where he went, though. I swear. All I know is that he works for Garcia Landscaping. Part-time. Trying to pay off his debts."

"Why'd you panic?" Silence said.

"Because Judkins owes to *everyone*, man. All over town. Everyone! I don't want no trouble with Toscani."

As soon as he said the name, his eyes instinctively flicked to the hypodermic, now several feet away, sitting in a pool of the muted light. It was some sort of bizarre Pavlovian response, the strung-out junkie version.

heroin = Toscani

Silence looked into the man's bloodshot eyes. He believed Snake. And he'd get nothing more from him.

"Thanks," he said and released the man's wrist.

Snake nodded, scratched at his track marks, and bit his lip again. Then he turned and shuffled off, disappearing into the trees behind the dumpsters.

The name played through Silence's mind.

Toscani.

Silence stepped over to the syringe, knelt down.

Those scratched-out symbols he'd seen on the end of the

barrel—the triangle, circle, and square—glistened in the streetlight.

He reached into his sport coat and retrieved his NedNotes brand PenPal notebook. PenPals were 5 x 3.5" and 100 pages thick with spiral binding—compact but substantial. Their plastic covers came in a variety of colors. This one was bright white with black flecks.

He took the mechanical pencil from the PenPal's spiral binding, flipped the notebook open, and tore out a page along the perforation.

Carefully avoiding the needle, he wrapped the paper around the syringe's barrel and gently brushed the pencil lead side to side, revealing the symbols beneath—their indentations showed as white marks in the shaded area.

After unrolling the paper, he double-checked his work. Satisfied, he tossed the syringe into the dumpster, turned, and left.

CHAPTER FIVE

THE AUDI ZOOMED DOWN the offramp, exiting Interstate 80. Ahead was the tower that had been Silence's home for the last three nights—the Horizon Palace Casino Resort, a luxury establishment in the heart of Reno's glitz, a polar opposite to the Silver Moon Motel he'd visited a few minutes earlier.

Part of Silence was resisting a sense of too-good-to-be-true. He'd been in Nevada—a state with a reputation for prostitution; a state that, since 1971, even had a limited number of legalized brothels—for three whole days, and his employers, the Watchers, *hadn't* sent him a prostitute.

Though the Watchers brass were a group of individuals who risked their lives, literally, for the sake of lessoning the ills of society, the ills they focused on were the big ones—murder, torture, human-trafficking, national security.

In terms of other ills like drugs and prostitution, the Watchers were not only lackadaisical, but they were also hypocritical. As an Asset—the title given to Watchers assassins—Silence had busted many prostitution rings when those organizations involved minors or when they abused people or when they dipped their toes into more heinous acts like murder.

But the same Watchers organization who sometimes had him risk his life to destroy prostitution rings also regularly sent prostitutes in his direction.

The Watchers were blatant and uncaring about this double-standard.

It made Silence despise them.

At least once or twice a year, they commissioned rendezvous for Silence. They recognized his eternal devotion to his dead fiancée, C.C., and they didn't like it. No Assets had spouses or children. Deep emotional bonds were detrimental to the mission. So they did their best to exterminate Silence's connection to C.C.

With hookers.

And Silence had thought for sure they'd send him one in Reno.

Three days in, nothing. So far, so good.

The Audi crunched to a stop under the porte cochère. A teen wearing a white dress shirt, black pants, and a gangly smile stepped up from behind the valet podium. Silence handed him the keys and a twenty.

He stood for a moment and watched the Audi roll off, glistening under the lights. He liked that car. It had been his for four months, but he'd only get two more months with it. Of the many fringe benefits of his position, Silence received free, brand-new vehicles, but the Watchers swapped them out every six months.

There was a bustling atmosphere on the brightly lit patio under the porte cochère, the air abuzz with the conversations of people embarking on a night amongst the city's many casinos. Laughter rippled through the area as people moved with purpose in and out the glass revolving doors of the luxury casino/hotel. Silence followed the flow of people going inside.

The lobby was modern—full of glass, slate, and other chic furnishings. An instrumental version of a pop song trickled through the room, and clusters of people headed toward the busy casino floor to the right. Outside the casino entrance, slot machines lined the walls of the lobby, which, like the classed-up pop song, leeched away some of the place's class.

Silence headed for the row of glistening brass elevator doors in the back of the space. His mind went to Donald Judkins. The Watchers' prodigious resources gave Silence distinct advantages as a manhunter, but it was often easier for him to track down well-off people than it was the forgotten ones, those with no set routine or address, particularly when those people were already on the run, hiding from self-manufactured demons.

But tracking an elusive individual often came with serendipitous encounters. He thought about the bizarre symbols he'd seen on the syringe back at the crappy motel. They must have meant something, but despite his copious training, cryptography was not a specialty of Silence's.

There was that person he'd thought of at the motel, the expert who could make sense of the symbols. But Silence wasn't going to contact that individual.

No. Not gonna happen.

Instead, there was another course of action, another person he could contact, though he didn't want to involve the second individual either. But this was the lesser of two evils.

One avoidant step at a time...

No matter what the symbols meant, the fact that they were on the syringes of tainted heroin meant they were somehow tied back to Demetrio Toscani, a man who cast an immense shadow over Reno, his tendrils of corruption spread far and wide.

He reminded himself again that Toscani wasn't his reason for being in Reno. He was there for the serial killer.

The Carver had killed three people so far, and if the police reports from the previous event were accurate, he'd recently killed a fourth. No one seemed to know who he was, and no one seemed to think he had any tie to Toscani or the new wave of heroin.

No one except a washed-out gambler.

No one except Donald Judkins.

A man Silence couldn't find.

Silence crossed the marble floor, and the tapping of his shoes was swallowed up into the excited din of his environment. There was a happy, anxious buzz to the place, the beginning of a gambling town evening. It was early yet, so there was no sense of desperation, no sense of panic, wishing and hoping and literally praying that the next roll of the dice was favorable, no drunken stumbling, no drunken vomiting. At that moment, everything was still optimistic. Pleasant, even. The night was wide open, and the opportunities were endless.

Just before the elevators, off the main floor, was the Nebula Lounge, a sleek bar with an ultra-modern aesthetic in a dim, brooding environment. Chrome features. Glowing blue accents and planes of glass. Behind the bar, a wall of illuminated liquor bottles stood out against the darkness.

As Silence passed by, he heard a light clatter of heels over the rest of the gentle buzz in the lobby. He turned.

A woman had just stepped out of Nebula's darkness, into the brighter light of the lobby floor, martini glass in hand. Stunningly beautiful. Deep dark skin, eyes, and hair. She wore a tight, short dress, and her body moved with fluid confidence as she followed Silence, making eye contact.

Shit.

Silence had jinxed himself by allowing his mind to drift into his thoughts of a few moments earlier.

Because as the woman approached, Silence recognized she

was a prostitute. Another high-class prostitute. The Watchers had sent him another companion.

He felt a wave of frustration. It was pointless to resist, so he slowed down to allow her to close the gap, but he turned away for a moment to compose himself.

When he turned back, she was right beside him.

"Hi," she said with a sweet smile. "Mr. Jones?"

Silence looked down at her. Blinked. Then nodded.

"My name's Lexi. I come with warm wishes from a Mr. Falcon."

Silence scoffed, but otherwise didn't respond.

Falcon was Silence's direct supervisor in the Watchers organization, his Prefect. Falcon was also the person who spearheaded the campaign of forced prostitution against Silence.

The sack of shit.

Lexi waited a moment longer for a response, and when Silence gave her none, she motioned to the elevators nearby and her voice softened.

"So ... you gonna invite me up?"

Silence hesitated.

"You'll be C.C. tonight," he said finally, his voice low and curt.

Lexi seemed confused, but she quickly recovered.

"You got it. C.C. it is," she said with a smile and a shrug.

Silence nodded and motioned for her to follow. They walked together to the elevators.

———

Later, Silence lay awake.

He was naked, on his back, fingers interlaced behind his head, staring at the ceiling of his luxury suite on the twelfth and top floor of the Horizon Palace Casino Resort tower.

The room was quiet, not even the hum of the air conditioner; he'd turned it off, as the nights had been chilly in Reno during his visit. There were just the faint sounds of nighttime revelry from the street far below. Earlier, Silence had mused that the energy of the people surrounding him had been optimistic, that the night hadn't yet succumbed to debauchery and desperation. From the whooping and the drunken laughter and the occasional shouts of anger below, it was apparent that the optimistic atmosphere had lost the good fight.

He let his mind drift into a meditation, a technique C.C. had taught him while he was still alive. The moments of absolute stillness were a brief reprieve from the pressure of his current reality.

For just a few seconds, he was able to concentrate on his touchpoints, on his breath, the feeling of it going through his nose, down his throat, filling his lungs, while everything went dark and soft...

But then his frustration swept the focus away. His body stirred, bringing him back to the present, and with it, the details of his expensively appointed room began to filter into his consciousness. He noticed the plush bedding and the oversized crystal vase, the lush carpets and the delicate gold frames on the walls, displaying artwork from around the world.

His gaze fell on the figure sleeping beside him. Lexi. Also naked. She lay peacefully on her side, her breath whistling in and out of her nose in a gentle rhythm. Her hand rested on his chest—a sign of purchased affection; the Watchers had paid for the "girlfriend experience"; they always did—and he realized that the hand must have gone there during his meditation. He hadn't noticed.

Guilt swelled within him, so suddenly that he felt it as a palpable force, and he swiped her hand away. It dropped onto the sheet with a light thump. The action caused Lexi to stir, to scrunch her face, but she did not wake.

This was bullshit. For years, the Watchers had done this—forced these women upon him. Each time, Silence used a secret weapon against his employers, fighting back against this undeserved punishment—he was able to use his overactive mind to visualize C.C. in the place of the woman he was having sex with.

But he often wondered—as he did now, staring up toward the texture of the suite's ceiling, up there in the darkness—if he was somehow deluding himself. In his previous existence, before the Watchers, before C.C.'s murder, he'd been ready to marry her, to promise himself to her for life. But it had been more than "till death do you part" for him. He had known he'd found his soulmate. While he made no judgement against people who cultivated love multiple times during their lives, he had known that he would never remarry should C.C. die before him.

And sadly, she was taken from him before their engagement had even come to fruition.

Murdered.

Destroyed face.

Flesh torn.

Blood. Lying in a puddle of blood that was still warm, just barely.

He wondered sometimes, though, if in some sick sort of way, these forced prostitution encounters were what gave him the strength to continue with his undying love for C.C.

Undoubtedly, these women were sating his primal, masculine need to release. Silence used his mind to imagine them as C.C.—he even had them refer to themselves as "C.C."—but did he completely fool himself?

Or did some part of him, somewhere buried deep down, *not* fall for the ruse?

And did that part enjoy the encounters?

Would he be able to continue loving C.C. the way he did without the prostitutes?

He gasped then, and his heartbeat raced.

If it weren't for the prostitutes, would Silence have the fortitude to make—

Quit it.

It was C.C.

Quit what? Silence's internal voice replied.

Quit thinking like that. Right now.

Silence took a moment.

But, C.C., what if they didn't push these women on me? Would I still be able to love you the way I—

C.C. cut in. *I heard what you thought a moment ago, and I told you to quit it.* She paused. *You love me, don't you?*

Of course.

And I love you. This doesn't need to make sense to anyone but you and me. And your situation is what it is. They force these women on you. You didn't ask for this.

Silence looked to his left. At Lexi. Hands stacked under her cheek. Dark hair splayed. Expensive makeup job, hardly disrupted.

I'm sorry, C.C.

I know, love.

They made me. I didn't ... I ... I didn't...

I know, love.

I'm so sorry.

Love! There was a pause. Then, quietly, she said, *Shhhh. Go to sleep.*

Silence released a long breath.

He gave another glance at Lexi, then looked up at the ceiling again.

Okay, he said.

He closed his eyes.

CHAPTER SIX

Ian Dalton stared out the window at a bleak view—his neighbor Hal's trailer.

Hal and two friends were out there this evening, drinking beer and telling stories in a trio of rickety lawn chairs, which sat in a half-circle around a campfire that illuminated their wretched, ignorant faces. Hal was a typical working-class guy, with a grizzled beard and dull eyes. Tonight, he wore his usual plaid shirt and suspenders. He laughed, throwing his head back. The laughter was clearly audible to Dalton, even across the distance and through the window.

Dalton detested that laugh. It was thunderous, grating, and piercing.

But Hal's horse laugh wasn't *entirely* revolting because it served an unintentional purpose. Whenever Dalton heard the irritating braying, it gave him a boost to keep going, to keep striving. Little by little, Dalton was repairing his life, and he couldn't break his momentum, no matter how often he felt stuck in place.

He wanted to get back to Los Angeles. *God,* he wished he was back there. It had been years since he lived in L.A.—

those days of pecking at his keyboard, sharing stories with colleagues, dreaming of cinematic adventures, meeting remarkable people. Dalton would get back to California through effort, dedication, sheer grit.

He could have his old life back.

With a swipe of the hand, he brushed the curtains back into place, wiping away the pathetic scene he'd been watching.

He was in the trailer's "master" bedroom. Wood paneling covered the walls. To his left, only inches from the desk where he sat, was a dresser. Just past that, filling the small room, was a queen-sized bed, its sheets and blanket twisted in a pile at the center. Dalton would have company in the bed tomorrow. That was a comforting thought, a bit of fun, a literal release of his built-up tension.

With his energy now refocused, with his priorities in order—*get out of this trailer; get out of this town; get back to L.A.*—he picked up the phone receiver, turn the rotary dial through a series of memorized digits.

It rang.

Outside, another belt of Hal's laughter carried through the glass, as if it was another punctuation to Dalton's resolve, another reminder.

Wallace Boyd answered the call.

"Dalton," the man said in his aging but commanding voice. "I hope you have some good news to share. It would be a pleasant change of pace."

Dalton hadn't said a word yet, and already Boyd was cutting into him, going at Dalton's command of the situation. He lifted his chin and took a calming breath before replying.

"I'm down to one," he said. "Only one box left to distribute. Garrity has been working on it this week."

Boyd didn't immediately respond. His distrust had been growing week by week. Lately, he did nothing to hide his utter lack of trust in Dalton and his assistant, Brooks Garrity. Dalton had met Boyd a few times in person, so he'd gotten a good feel for the man's temperament—all business, shrewd but optimistic, never downbeat. As such, getting such speculative treatment from a man of this nature felt dangerous.

Ominous, even.

Finally, Boyd said, "That would sound promising to me, were it not for the fact that your man is on the news every day—the mysterious Carver killer, the more talked-about of Reno's dual threats."

Dalton pressed forward. The best a person could do when confronted with a force of nature like Wallace Boyd was to show unrelenting progress toward one's goals.

"There are only six more syringes to distribute," Dalton said. "You have not a thing to be concerned about, Boyd. Our operation won't be compromised because of one man's incompetence. I can shorten Brooks Garrity's leash."

For a moment, Dalton almost didn't have the nerve to continue with what he needed to say next. It was risky business, being even slightly confrontational with Boyd. But for the operation to continue, there was a question that Dalton simply had to ask.

"The syringes," Dalton said. "You told me you got them locally..."

To soften the impact, he let his sentence fade off—an implied question, not a genuine question.

Again, there was a delay before Boyd responded, and when he did, he let his response trail off in the same way that Dalton's statement had. "Yes..."

"They have markings. Hand-drawn. I'm concerned that could tie them back to us."

Another pause. "That *is* concerning. But it's the risk you take when you're using hot items. If anything, it'll tie them back to the place we yanked them from, not to us."

"Nonetheless, I'm having Garrity look into it," Dalton said. "This will give him purpose, too. Something to get his mind off his sick fantasies. I *can* reel him in, Boyd."

Dalton winced as soon as he'd finished his sentence. There had been desperation in his tone, subservience. Pathetic.

Boyd exhaled. "I'll inform the partners of your reassurances, but it won't be enough to ease their concerns. I've been asked to inform you that we're meeting with you. Tomorrow."

For a moment, Dalton couldn't respond. His heart raced.

This wasn't the agreed-upon arrangement. Aside from Boyd, the other business partners had wanted to remain anonymous. This had been a nonnegotiable component of the original agreement. The fact that *they* wanted to change the parameters with zero cajoling from Dalton was immensely concerning.

However, the notion only fretted Dalton for a moment before hubris and pride wiped it away. He sucked in a frustrated breath and fought the urge to lash out at Boyd. Dalton *despised* being told what to do, and the man had presented the upcoming meeting as requisite.

Still, Dalton knew that the whole of the operation rested on the business partners' input—and their millions of dollars. They had Dalton by the short hairs. So, like a subservient wretch, he managed to say, "Absolutely, Mr. Boyd. In person?"

"That's right. In person and in public."

"If that's what the partners want."

"Not just the other partners—I'm getting nervous too, Mr. Dalton," Boyd said, his tone darkening even more. "I don't trust your man, Brooks Garrity. He's jeopardizing everything."

"I can handle him. A few more syringes. Then it's done.

And I made it clear tonight that he's finished with his killings. He's under control now."

"I hope you're right."

The line went dead. Dalton slowly lowered the receiver back onto the cradle.

Through the thin drapery covering the window in front of him, he saw movement. He stuck a finger in the curtains and pulled them back. Outside, a pickup truck came to a stop in front of his neighbor's trailer. The men seated by the fire greeted the newcomer boisterously, though none of them pulled their fat asses out of their decrepit chairs.

The one who oozed out of the truck was just like the others—fat, jovial, slovenly. He held a six-pack aloft—displaying it with pride and an idiot smile—and lumbered over to his friends, took a seat.

Dalton felt a grin form on his lips.

Every time he got to worrying about his operation, he reminded himself that the majority of modern society was worthless scum. In that sense, the lunatic Brooks Garrity was on to something with his desire to cull the population of degenerates. It didn't take much to succeed in the world today. To confirm this notion, to reassert his confidence and to tame any worries that might arise, all Dalton had to do was look out his back window at Hal's trailer.

Morons like those in front of him were his ticket out of this life.

Dalton just had to take care of a few more complications.

CHAPTER SEVEN

THE WOMAN GAVE SILENCE A LOOK. "Well, this is a change—you *requesting* to see me."

Silence didn't respond.

She stood at the threshold of his suite, bathed in pinkish morning sunlight streaming into the hallway through its copious windows.

Doc Hazel—the mental health professional the Watchers had assigned to Silence years ago. He had never requested counseling, but his wishes had always been of little consequence to his employers, so Doc Hazel had become a regular presence, one of only a handful of constancies in Silence's life.

She was right. It *was* unusual for him to request a meeting with her. In a way, he was as confused as she was.

Doc Hazel blinked from behind a pair of designer glasses as she craned to look up at him. The stilettos she wore added a few inches to her taller-than-average stature, yet she still had to lean back to glance up at Silence's six-foot-three stature. The tightness of her professional ponytail accented the angular contours of her face, and the long, toned legs stretching out of her suit skirt were bare, glistening in all that morning sunlight.

Silence stepped aside and gestured for her to enter. Without hesitation, she breezed past him, heels clicking on the marble flooring, seemingly unaffected by the lavish surroundings. Silence watched her with a faint smirk. She walked with immaculate posture and the precision and speed of an important professional. A gust of her perfume washed over him—vanilla, patchouli, bergamot.

Silence followed her through the suite—the marble finishes, the soft colors, and the modern furniture. He took a seat on a sofa. Doc Hazel sat opposite him in an armchair across the glass table.

She watched him for a moment. There was the faint murmur of traffic passing by twelve stories below, the hum of the refrigerator behind them.

Doc Hazel remained expressionless as her eyes blinked slowly a couple of times. Finally, she said, "Did you enjoy the companion we sent you? Lexi, was it?"

This woman was his mental health professional, yes, but she was also a Specialist, one of Silence's innumerable superiors in the Watchers, and as such, she knew all about the challenges the organization placed in Silence's way. They were all in on it, this seemingly endless attempt to torment him.

That's why she was asking about Lexi.

Silence didn't respond.

Doc Hazel watched, waited, blinked, and ultimately rolled her eyes. Silence was surprised that someone could make a roll of the eyes look not only mechanical but also professional. Doc Hazel had pulled it off. She bore a permanent expression of flat impassivity, even when offering snotty nonverbals.

"I hope you understand that hypnotherapy is not my area

of expertise," she said as she opened her attaché case and searched inside.

Silence grunted in the affirmative.

She had stated it matter-of-factly, as though he should already understand that she wasn't versed in hypnosis.

But the truth was, Silence didn't know *anything* about her expertise, her credentials. He'd often wondered if she was a mental health professional at all. He had a strong suspicion that her day job was that of an actress, and her hazel-colored eyes supported this notion; since she went by the pseudonym of Doc Hazel, the name seemed almost like another mind game from the Watchers. It certainly fit the bill.

Doc Hazel retrieved a notebook and a handheld tape-player from the bag.

"Let's begin," she said and motioned to the sofa Silence where Silence was seated. She wanted him to lie down, a mainstay of their counseling sessions. Silence hadn't been sure if he would need to recline for a hypnosis session as well. Now he had his answer.

He lay down.

This wasn't entirely new territory for him. Silence was well familiar with being hypnotized. When his esoteric fiancée was still alive, C.C. had led him through a few hypnosis sessions. And back in his house in Pensacola, Florida, Silence had a sensory deprivation chamber, also known as a floating pod. Many of his sessions in the pod felt much like hypnosis.

Silence stared at the ceiling, which was as immaculate as the rest of the suite.

There was a *click* from the tape-player, and a soothing white noise played.

"I'm going to count down," Doc Hazel said. "You'll get more relaxed with each number. Three—your legs melting into the sofa."

His legs relaxed, going limp, the backs of his thighs sinking into the sofa as requested, feeling heavy.

"Two, getting heavier..."

Yes, heavier.

"One, completely at ease, completely gone."

Gone.

Silence was detached.

Darkness before his eyes.

"You're in the past, now," Doc Hazel's voice said from a distance. "Back in Spokane, Washington, two and a half years ago."

Out of the darkness, Spokane appeared. Just a tiny portion of it.

The loading dock at the back of the warehouse. Night. Spitting rain. Everything glistened wet.

"What do you see?"

Silence looked left, right. Nothing. Just pavement. And the rubber mats. A truck. He was looking for a person, and...

There.

There she was.

"I see..." Silence said and swallowed. "Cerise Hillman. To my left."

Cerise. Eyes wide. Dread. Red hair billowing behind her, reaching out from the darkness.

"Yes, that's correct," Doc Hazel's voice echoed. "Hillman was there. Right before it happened. And what is she doing right now?"

Silence turned a bit more. The darkness was closing in, a tunnel of black, an iris squeezing out this fraction of a memory. He concentrated, forcing it to linger.

"She's..." Silence said and trailed off, focusing even more intently. "She's screaming. Coming toward me."

Cerise was sprinting right at him. Long trench coat, open in the front, belt flapping behind her on either side. Plush lips spread in a wide O as she yelled out to him. Hand outstretched, fingers spread, reaching in vain.

"Then?" Doc Hazel said.

Silence turned.

...and saw a flash of movement.

"The bat," he said.

There was Culverson—his pig face wet with rain; his upturned pig snout of a nose; his buzz-cut hair—materialized from behind the truck.

He was supposed to be gone. Dammit, intel had said Culverson was on the other side of the freaking country!

He was supposed to be in Vermont.

There was no reason, not an inkling of a notion of an idea in Silence's mind that Culverson would be there at the loading dock in Spokane.

But there he was.

With a metal baseball bat.

Silence had heard him. But not in time. The bat came at his head.

"Then?" Doc Hazel said again.

"Pain."

A searing pain. Through Silence's entire body.

Silence had sharper reflexes than almost anyone—but Culverson wasn't just anyone. He was one of the most highly trained martial artists Silence had faced, and his speed was staggering.

And he wasn't supposed to be there.

With no other weapons available, Culverson had improvised with a baseball bat.

And Silence had taken its brunt.

"I'm falling," Silence said.

He saw Cerise screaming, reaching for him, sprinting. A puddle splashed under her boot.

Silence's body twisted as he collapsed, changing his angle,

revealing the clattering bat on the wet concrete and Culverson bolting away, going smaller, feet churning, gone.

Rain drops spattered Silence's cheek. Cold.

Then there was heat. On the opposite cheek. Warmth spreading, overtaking the frigid blacktop pressed against his face. Blood.

"He's gone," Silence said, swallowed. "Escaped. But I still killed him."

The loading dock flashed into nothingness, its darkness whisked away to reveal bright interior lighting that glistened off highly polished metal and tile.

Culverson.

Buck-naked.

In a luxury bathtub. Black tile. Slate. Chrome accents. One arm extended, reaching toward Silence, pleading.

Culverson's hand was just like Cerise's had been the previous evening—reaching for Silence, anxious, fingers outstretched, dappled with water droplets.

Silence raised his suppressed Beretta. He fired twice into Culverson's forehead.

Hot blood spattered Silence's fingers.

"Go back a day, back to the critical moment," Doc Hazel said. "Back to the warehouse."

The wet concrete. Cold against Silence's cheek, going warm as the puddle of blood expanded beneath his face.

Cerise kneeling before him.

Her hand went to his forehead.

"My God!" she screamed. "*Oh my God!*"

"What else?" Doc Hazel said.

Her hand.

"Her hand," Silence said and swallowed. "On my forehead." Another swallow. "Then on my shoulder."

Groaning, Silence used all his energy to shift his eyes upward. He saw Cerise's hand. On his shoulder. Dappled with rain. Fingers tight. Clenching the wet cloth of his jacket.

Her hand.

Her hand on his shoulder...

Earlier in the mission. Before the incident.

The previous night. It was dark, difficult to see. Her hand was on his shoulder. The exact same position and once more dappled with moisture.

His shoulder was bare.

"Why does it have to be this way?" Cerise said.

The room was shadowy, and the vision grew darker, darker, until she was gone.

"Go on," Doc Hazel said.

Silence focused, squinting his internal attention, and an outline of Cerise reappeared—just a vague ghost figure, standing before him, in a T-shirt. looking up at him as he stepped away from her.

"No," he'd told Cerise.

And then, in the present, he told Doc Hazel, "Cerise is right in front of me."

"And?"

"And... and..."

Darkness consumed his vision, the iris squeezing tight once more until there was nothing. An utter black void. A sense of finality.

Silence's eyes snapped open. The ceiling was above him. Spotless, clean. The luxury hotel suite.

He gulped.

"And then nothing," he said.

"Interesting," Doc Hazel said. There was the sound of a pen going to work on her notebook.

"And what did you find in this regression?" she said. "Anything that might help?"

"No."

"Cerise Hillman is an expert cryptographer," Doc Hazel said. "*You* contacted *me* for a hypnosis session to try to dig up memories from your amnesia, something from Cerise's work two and a half years ago during your Spokane mission that might help here in Reno. They're *your* memories, Suppressor," she continued, using his codename, Suppressor, "which means *you* need to put in the work. Really think. *Really* concentrate. What did Hillman tell you during the previous mission that might help?"

Echoing Doc Hazel's sentiments, C.C.'s voice came to him. *Focus, love. You can do this. See through the amnesia.*

Silence squinted his eyes. And tried. He tried hard.

Damn hard.

Cerise. In a T-shirt. The pain on her face.

A different moment. A different expression. Fear. She wore a wet trench coat. Running toward him. Screaming.

Her hand on his shoulder, fingers twisted in his jacket.

The bat. Culverson's pig face.

Cerise's hand. On his bare shoulder.

She wore a T-shirt. The pain on her face.

"Why does it have to be this way?"

"I ... I can't remember," Silence said and swallowed. "All jumbled."

"Interesting." More pen scratches "Open your eyes in three, two, one."

Silence's eyes opened.

"I suppose that concludes our first-ever hypnosis session, Suppressor."

Silence pulled his legs off the sofa and sat up, faced her. He stretched.

Without taking her downcast attention off her notebook, Doc Hazel said, "I didn't tell you to get up."

Silence scowled at her. She didn't see it, though; her head was still downcast as she continued scribbling away.

He lay back down and resumed his view of the ceiling.

A few more pen scratches, then Doc Hazel said, "Since I'm here, we're still going to have one of our sessions." She cleared her throat. "Tell me, are you still talking to Cecilia?"

Doc Hazel always used the full name "Cecilia," even though she knew full well that Silence called his fiancée "C.C." It was another subtle power move, another means of keeping the Asset in his administratively assigned place. She regularly questioned him about C.C., and she made it a point to criticize the fact that Silence communicated with her in his head.

He wished he'd never told her in the first place.

"Yes, ma'am."

"Hmm," she said as her pen scratched. "Since you're continuing to hold these conversations against my wishes and my counsel, tell me, do you feel they're of benefit to you?"

Silence gave this some thought. He'd never even debated whether his talks with the shadow version of C.C. in his head were of benefit or not. To him, the voice of C.C. in his head was a part of his fiancée that would never die. The only part.

Of course it was a good thing that he talked to C.C. What a stupid question.

"Yes," he said.

"Hmm," Doc Hazel said again. Her pen scratching stopped, and there was a *thump* as she placed her pen on the notebook. "I have to cut this short. Got a flight to catch. And by the way, just because we had an impromptu session doesn't mean you're getting out of your scheduled session next month."

Great...

"You can sit up now," she said.

He did so.

Doc Hazel had her arms crossed over her crossed legs, leaning toward him—a slightly more relaxed posture.

"Don't be surprised if more memories come back," she said. "Some of them might have been physically expelled, but others might be repressed. We could have dislodged a few of them in the hypnotherapy. In the meantime, I'm going to take more proactive measures to help with your mission."

Silence was pretty sure he understood what she meant by that.

But he didn't respond.

"Donald Judkins—you mentioned that you finally got a lock on him," Doc Hazel said. "He's desperate. Desperate people are elusive. Just remember that desperation brings out the absolute worst in people, but it can also bring out the best."

She stood and turned. Silence followed her across the suite and opened the door for her.

In the doorway, she stopped and stared up at him. They were back in the positions where they'd been a few minutes earlier when she'd arrived.

"Good luck, Suppressor," she said. It was the standard well-wishing that Watchers higher-ups offered Assets shouldering another life-threatening mission.

She left.

CHAPTER EIGHT

FOR MONTHS NOW, Don Judkins had done a damn good job of avoiding the numerous people around the city who wanted to break his thumbs ... or worse.

He'd been able to stay one step ahead of them. He'd managed to stay off their radar.

So now he felt mostly safe with his decision: to sate his growling stomach here in a crowded, outdoor cafe, loaded with tourists in the heart of downtown.

The sun shone through the bright blue sky, and the bustling outdoor patio was full of laughter and clinking glasses, the kind of atmosphere one would expect from a highly rated and popular restaurant in the heart of an iconic gambling town. Each wrought-iron table was occupied with tourists in T-shirts and polos and sundresses, enjoying the warm weather, sharing stories of successes and failures at the casinos.

He was seated at one of the tables. A single daisy was in a vase at its center, upright but leaning, a bit like Don's current struggles. He had barely had time to admire it when he heard a congenial voice calling out to him. A waiter was striding in his direction, a welcoming smile on his face.

The waiter approached Don, ready to take his order.

"Good afternoon! Can I start you off with something to—"

Don quickly cut him off.

"A BLT, water, and make it fast," he spat out.

The waiter raised an eyebrow, visibly taken aback by Don's abruptness. But he scribbled down the order and hurried away.

Don watched him leave, but quickly came back to the dark reality of his life, and he couldn't help but scope out the surrounding tables. Everywhere he went in town, he felt he was being watched, tracked by all the debtors to whom he owed money. He had been on the run for weeks—no, it was *months* now—living off whatever he could get his hands on and sleeping wherever he could, always looking over his shoulder.

But for now, he was safe. He took in a breath, held it, released. This was supposed to calm one's nerves—deep breathing. It was yoga or New Age or some such shit. Whatever it was, it did help, admittedly. He'd been using it off and on in recent days.

Yes, Don was safe. For just a few moments, he would allow himself a minor indulgence, something nicer than McDonald's burgers and gas station burritos, the subsistence of a man on the run, trapped in his own city.

The sun felt good, melting away some of the tension in his face. He sensed his cheeks slacken. Yes, he would enjoy this. Just twenty minutes. Some real food would help him to recharge, to get his head on straight so he could plan his next move.

That was when the man approached out of nowhere and sat right across from him.

A big man.

Huge.

The iron chair on the other side of the table scratched heavily on the brickwork as the man pulled it out. He plopped down into the chair and stared at Don from behind a pair of expensive sunglasses. Don recognized them. You don't become a professional gambler without learning to identify sunglass manufacturers. This man wore Versace.

Don's heart thundered, and he winced, expecting a knife or a gun or...

Nothing.

The man just stared at him.

The guy was enormous, which amplified Don's fear. Well over six feet tall. Broad-shouldered. Dark hair, dark complexion. Angular features that cast deep shadows in the bright sunlight. Exotic and foreign-looking.

The man seemed to sense Don's fear. He stared at Don with a blank expression, a look that almost seemed to say: *I know why you're running. I know what you owe. I'm here to collect.*

Don tried his best to keep his cool, but he knew that any wrong move could mean his life. He stared back at the man, anticipating the retrieval of that weapon he'd conjured in his mind a moment earlier.

And the man didn't disappoint; he reached into his sport coat.

Don winced.

But the man retrieved a wallet, not a pistol. From the wallet, he took out a keycard and reached it across the table.

Don stared. Didn't move. The man just kept his hand extended halfway across the tabletop, the card pinched between his fingers.

Finally, with a shaky hand, Don took it.

It wasn't a keycard. There was no magnetic strip on the back. It was just a blank plastic card of the same shape and dimensions as a keycard or credit card. It was primarily opaque, with one side covered by blue angular designs. Blue, raised lettering gave a message:

MY ORGANIZATION IS AWARE OF YOUR SITUATION.

WE UNDERSTAND NORMAL CHANNELS HAVE FAILED YOU.

WE HAVE THE MEANS TO ASSIST.

PLEASE EXCUSE THIS FORM OF INTRODUCTION.

I AM NOT MUTE, BUT SPEAKING IS PAINFUL.

I AM HERE TO HELP.

Don looked up, mouth gaping.

This man wasn't some tough from the back-room, unsanctioned casinos. He wasn't a gun-for-hire. He wasn't associated with Don's debts at all.

"Wait," Don said. "Is this about my talking to the Reno police?

The man nodded. He held out his hand, palm up. A moment later, Don took his meaning and returned his card.

"What is the 'organization' you're with?" Don said. "Like, the feds?"

The man didn't respond, just put the card back in his wallet and returned the wallet to his sport coat.

"What's your name?" Don said.

"Max."

The man's voice made Don jump back in his seat. It was horrendous and deep, crackling. Just awful. Almost unreal.

It took Don a few seconds before he could reply. He gulped and said, "But you're here to help me?"

Max nodded.

"How do I know you're not with my, um ... creditors?"

Max didn't respond.

Don thought this through. "I guess those folks would have no way of knowing I went to the police, huh?"

Max gave a nod and a slight grin of satisfaction that Don had put two and two together.

"Talk," Max said.

Don hesitated. "As long as you'll help my friend."

Max nodded. "I will."

Don bit his lip, ran a finger along the loops of iron that formed the tabletop.

"Okay, listen," he said finally. "Everyone thinks Reno has two tragedies—the Carver and the drug ODs. But I know they're one and the same."

"How know that?" Max said and swallowed hard.

The overt swallowing and the broken English—*How know that?*—must have been techniques Max used to soothe the throat condition that his card mentioned.

"Because my friend Kendall Anson works at Garcia Landscaping with me. Our shift supervisor is connected to it all. Ian Dalton. She told me he's trying to compete with Demetrio Toscani, the mob boss. Since heroin is the drug that's been killing all those people, the media and the cops are tying it to Toscani. But they're wrong."

"How would Anson..." Max said and swallowed. "Know that?"

Again, Don hesitated. "Because she, um ... has a special tie to Ian Dalton. A personal one. Outside of the landscaping company. She overheard him talking on the phone about distributing heroin and how it was the heroin causing the ODs."

Max shrugged. "Maybe he works for Toscani..." He swallowed. "On the side."

"No, Kendall said that during the phone call, Dalton talked *about* Toscani. And Dalton has been my supervisor at Garcia for a year now. Trust me, he's not the type that a man like Demetrio Toscani would hire."

Something sparkled in Max's dark eyes, and it was clear that he was ruminating on the details Don had offered. Max's visage had also lit up slightly a few moments earlier with Don's careful choice of words—"special tie"—when describing Kendall's connection to Dalton. It had been Don's attempt at maintaining his friend's privacy.

For now...

He was certain he would need to tell Max eventually, but Max seemed not overly anxious to press the issue. Don recognized this man was a thinker and a shrewd son of a bitch. As sneaky—hell, slimy—as Don could be, he wouldn't be able to pull the wool over this guy's eyes like he had so many others. He would have to play it extremely safe.

Max reached into his sport coat and took out a small, chunky notebook. The front cover was plastic. Bright white with black flecks. It looked like Breyer's vanilla ice cream, the natural kind. Max flipped the notebook open, took out a folded page that had already been removed from the spiral binding, and handed it across the table.

Don looked at it. In the center of the page was a patch of pencil scratchings. White shapes in the scratches revealed writing. This was a technique Don had seen before in spy movies—where someone places a paper over the indentations of past writing and shades the area to reveal what had been written there.

Max's pencil scratchings revealed three hand-drawn shapes: a triangle, a circle, and a square. They were small, about an eighth of an inch squared each.

"Recognize symbols?" Max said.

Don shook his head, totally perplexed.

Max reached his hand across the table, palm-up as he had before, and Don returned the paper.

"They're on the syringes," Max said and swallowed as he put the paper back in the notebook and returned the notebook to his pocket. "What's the link between..." Another swallow. "Drugs and serial killer?"

"I ... I think. It's Brooks Garrity, Dalton's hanger-on. Garrity follows Dalton around like a big brother. He works for Garcia Landscaping as well."

"Kendall told you that, too?" Max said and swallowed. "That Garrity is the Carver?"

"No. I put that part together myself. Hear me out. Garrity's a certified creep, all right? One time we all went out for beers after a big job—a total re-haul at a hospital—shrubbery, sod, trees, the whole works. Me and Garrity were the last two at the bar. Garrity had too much to drink and really opened up to me, just yanked open the floodgates. Told me he had this fantasy of cutting people up. *With a knife!* He told me that, man! The guy's white, twenties, dark blond hair, just like the Carver's description. And Garrity's idol, Dalton, is connected to the drugs..."

He trailed off for a moment, looking Max right in the eye.

"I mean, it *has* to be Garrity. Come on! I went to the police, but they didn't trust me, not with my reputation, not with all the trouble I've gotten in across town. The only reason I'm still breathing is that all my creditors are balancing each other out—no one wants to kill someone who owes a debt to one of their competitors. Not the sort of places I owe money to, anyway. I guess it's sort of a gentleman's agreement."

Max pointed to the towers surrounding them. "Which casinos?"

"My debts aren't with any official casino."

Max blinked. "Toscani?"

"No! Hell no! I've at least been smart enough to stay away from Toscani, thank God. Otherwise, there would be no gentleman's agreement; I'd be dead already. He holds all the power in town. He's not worried about anyone else."

Don took another one of those deep yoga breaths and sighed it out.

"No, I got in deep with backroom stuff. High-stakes. I do pretty good at the casinos, but I freakin' *clean up* at the unsanctioned stuff. Well, I *used to* clean up, until I, um ... faltered. I mean, you mess up once, and you're, like, *All I have to do is win* one *of the next three rounds. That'll take me back to even, then I'll leave.* But then you don't win in the next round. You don't win in the next *dozen* rounds. Then you try somewhere else, somewhere to pay off the first place, and you lose there too. Then, you ... you..."

He stopped.

Suddenly, this felt wrong. He was sharing too much. Even if Max was truly there to help—as his card claimed—Don had much more pressing matters to consume his time. Sure, Don wanted to help Kendall, but he had to save his own skin first.

And something told Don that this mysterious big man from a mysterious "organization" was fully on the side of righteousness. As such, Max might very well want to use Don to get to the bottom of the Carver/heroin connection...

...and then turn him over to the enforcers.

Again, Don thought of guns. Knives. Broken thumbs. Or drowning. Don had always feared drowning, and some of these guys were rumored to tie you up in chains, drop you in the Truckee River, just deep enough, inches below the surface, face-up, so you could stare helplessly at air and life and sunlight while you slowly panicked, until you could take it no longer, opened your mouth, and water flooded into your lungs.

Yeah, to hell with this. Don wasn't taking any chances. Screw this Max guy.

The waiter appeared in the distance, over Max's shoulder.

Don glanced at the waiter, forced a big smile, and waved. When Max turned to see who Don had acknowledged...

...Don bolted.

CHAPTER NINE

THE ROTTEN HUMANITY surrounding Brooks was so thick he could *smell* it.

Perfume and cologne. Cigarette smoke. Alcohol. Sweat.

It was a stench. Awful. As putrid as the people who'd spawned it.

Brooks walked through downtown Reno. It was noon, and while the area wasn't terribly crowded, there were still plenty of people out and about, going into the shops and bars. Some of them were clearly drunk already. Brooks watched them as he strolled, and he wished them all gone. Far gone. As far away from him as possible.

He turned a corner and stepped into a small shop with a large sign announcing itself as *Quick Stop*. It was a typical convenience store. Brightly lit and filled with aisles of snacks and price-gouged essentials. In back, a humming wall of built-in coolers lined with drinks. To the left, a hotdog case slowly spinning its wares on stainless steel rollers.

It was grimier than most convenience stores, and as Brooks stepped toward the rear of the store, the soles of his boots stuck to the linoleum. There was a reason it was less than spotless: the store was a front.

An Indian woman in a blue uniform bearing the Quick Stop logo was in the back behind a counter. Light brown hair, salt-and-pepper hair tied back in a neat bun. Her eyes sparkled when she smiled at Brooks, and she stacked her hands on the counter in front of her as she waited for him to approach.

This was her?

This was Calypso?

It had taken Brooks three days—three days of searching, of slinking around casinos and rotten, putrid hell hole sides of town, and this fat Indian chick was the woman of so much esteem?

Brooks walked through the center of the store, ignoring the items surrounding him, and approached her, maintaining eye contact. The woman gave a smile, and Brooks forced a return smile to his face.

"May I help you?" the woman said in a thick accent.

"Maybe," Brooks said and pointed to her name tag. "But I'm not looking for Divya. I'm looking for a woman with an entirely different name."

Instantly, the woman's warm, professional facade vanished. Darkness swept over her face, and a coy smile brought one corner of her lips up.

"Oh?" she said. "And who are you looking for?"

"See, I've been asking a few questions around town," Brooks said. "It took me a while, but every question brought me a little further ahead, step by step, until I got to this lil ol' convenience store." He paused. "I'm looking for Calypso."

The woman's face darkened even more, and her sneer grew even larger. Brooks had known some wicked folks, and even from a first impression, Calypso was right there at the top of the list.

Soulless eyes.

She watched him for a moment. Then she reached under the counter. There was a small *beep* from below, followed immediately by a mechanical buzz several feet away. Brooks looked. The camera in the corner had shut off.

Calypso's hands returned with a ledger—just a small organizer. Such an innocuous, simple-looking thing, yet Brooks had heard about it all over town: Calypso's little black book.

"What is it you seek?" Calypso said, a finger tracing along the book slowly, almost sensually. "Pussy? Or something a little stronger? Blow? Stardust? Or maybe the good stuff, some of Toscani's?"

Brooks shook his head. "I'm looking for information."

Calypso raised an eyebrow. "Oh?"

"I've heard you barter secrets as well as you do vices."

Calypso gave a shrug that said *You got me*, which only amplified her wicked grin.

"What do you know about symbols?" Brooks said.

She looked at him for a long moment, and the dark strength in her face strained for the first time. "Symbols?"

Brooks felt a bit of a power switch. He had something on her. "Yes, symbols. You know what I'm asking about. I can see it in your eyes."

Calypso didn't respond. Her nostrils flared.

Finally, she said, "I barter in sundry pieces of information, but symbols aren't one of them. I need to ask you to leave."

Brooks didn't budge. "Cut the shit. The new heroin—the syringes have markings scratched in their barrels. What do the symbols mean? Where did they come from?"

Suddenly, the last trace of bravado on Calypso's face vanished as her eyes went wide. Her strength was replaced by fear.

"I ... I don't know. Just rumors. All I know is the ones with the octagon symbol are deadliest and that whoever is dumping those drugs is going directly against Toscani. I don't want to cross Toscani. Not in any way. I ... I really need to ask you to leave."

Of course, it was Brooks himself she was talking about—the man who was dumping the new heroin into the streets on behalf of Ian Dalton. Naturally, he wasn't going to tell her that, but he had spent a good deal of energy tracking her down, because if there was anyone in town who knew about the rumors of the symbols, it was the infamous Calypso, a fable of a woman with her finger in all the pies.

Yet it was exceedingly evident from her expression that even *she* didn't know what the symbols meant. Obviously, she had heard the rumors—and one specifically about octagons—but Brooks would get no further explanation from her, no deciphering of the code, no details on the origin of the syringes that he and Dalton were distributing.

The octagon information was interesting, however. With all the syringes he'd distributed, Brooks he hadn't seen an octagon. Could he have missed something?

"Tell me more about the octagons. Where do they fall in the sequences?"

"I know no more than that. I swear! I told you everything."

There was something strange about Calypso's overall reaction. Why had her confidence vanished so suddenly? And why was she afraid? The Calypso of legend, the woman he'd been tracking down for three days, was supposedly afraid of no one; that's how she'd become such a significant player.

But Calypso had suddenly gone terrified.

And with a burst of realization, Brooks thought he understood why...

Shit!

His heart rate quickened.

Immediately, though, he composed himself and chose a

new course of action. If he had faltered, then he had to get the most out of this encounter.

And then decide how to cut his losses.

"Rumors," he said. "You mentioned 'rumors.' Tell me, Calypso, what are the latest rumors on the street?"

"I don't know anymore than you! I swear!" she said. "They're saying the syringes have symbols, little markings on the top that—"

"Not *those* rumors," Brooks said in a deadly tone. "Not the drugs. The *other* rumors, those concerning the serial killer. Tell me what you've heard, Calypso. What's the word around town?"

Her eyes lingered on him.

"They say the Carver..." she said and trailed off. Her voice was ragged now, barely a whisper. "They say he's not only killing people. They say he's been going around town asking about the symbols on the new drugs' syringes."

A cold sweat flashed over Brooks's skin.

It was as he'd feared.

He *had* messed up. He'd been careless again. *Foolish.*

Now Calypso, one of the most well-connected people in the Reno underworld, had met the Carver face-to-face. She could ID him.

And she understood that there was a connection between the serial killer and the city's influx of new drugs.

Brooks's concern turned to pure panic. But he kept his tone and his composure icy cold. "The Carver, huh?"

Calypso nodded.

"The cops don't know what the guy looks like," Brooks said. "But there are rumors on the street. The great Calypso has heard the rumors, no doubt."

She nodded again.

"And what does the Carver look like, Calypso?"

Her lips parted, and a small puttering sound came out before her words formed.

"White ... dark blond hair ... brown eyes."

Her eyes instinctively traced over Brooks's corresponding physical features as she listed them off.

By now, there was no point in trying to hide anything. In fact, he needed to use it to his advantage. So he gave the woman a dark stare and said, "You're *sure* you don't know anything about the symbols?"

Calypso nodded, trembling.

"Well, if you do, I want to know," he said. "I'll be back. Pleasure meeting you."

He turned and walked away, keeping his head low in case she immediately fired up her security cameras again.

The bell rattled, and he was back in the sunlight, back in the Reno revelry—the laughter, the smell of alcohol. He put on his sunglasses and left.

He'd clearly frightened the woman, yes. But that was of no consequence now.

Because she knew.

She knew the connections, and now she knew his face.

This was troubling. Extremely troubling.

Brooks had already messed things up so badly. He couldn't imagine how Dalton would react if he knew what had just happened with Calypso.

Brooks thought about what he'd just told the woman— that he would be back to get more information out of her.

Brooks would return to the Quick Stop, all right.

But it would be for an entirely different reason.

CHAPTER TEN

DON SHOVED his way past the patrons in the outdoor cafe, feeling the presence of the large man behind him in pursuit. His heart pounded, and his breath came in short gasps. All around him, the cafe's customers cut themselves off mid-conversation to watch dumbfounded as he weaved through the space, shoving his way past waiters and gawkers.

He stumbled through the tables and chairs, narrowly avoiding collisions as he went. Max's footsteps pounded behind him, and Don picked up the pace, but still the other man seemed to gain. Ahead, his pathway closed, as the back wall of the restaurant was coming up fast—windows showing white tablecloths and more wide-eyed, pointing customers.

Suddenly, a gap opened up in the crowd, and Don made for it. As he passed through, he felt a rush of relief. This could be his pathway out of this. It was a dim chance, but it was a chance, nonetheless.

He whipped around the corner and found himself in a narrow alleyway. He ducked behind a dumpster and held his breath, listening for Max's footsteps. But all he heard was the sound of his own pounding heart.

He waited for what seemed like an eternity before he dared to peek out from behind the dumpster. When he finally did, he saw that the alley was empty. Max was gone.

Don let out a sigh of relief. He was safe.

But he couldn't stay there forever. He doubled-checked—still no Max—then crept out from behind his cover and made his way toward the nearest building, stealing a glance behind him.

Still nothing.

He slowed his pace. He knew that ahead, about half a block, was a small pathway that would take him to Sierra Street. From there, he would pull a couple of turns that only a local would know, and then there would be no way that Max could trail him.

He turned a corner.

And yelled.

There was Max.

He swooped out of nowhere, from behind a wall. It didn't seem possible, but somehow Max had not only caught up with Don but overtaken him.

Max looked down at him. His face was still as robotic, as stoic as it had been back at the cafe, but now there was something burning in his eyes. Don could see that clearly, as Max had taken off his sunglasses since the two of them had run off.

Don's heart thundered, and his breath caught in his throat. He had nowhere to turn, nowhere to run. There was no path in the tiny alley Max was blocking—just a brick wall on either side of him. If Don pivoted and tried to bolt off in the direction from which he'd come, Max would surely grab him. The man had already displayed how unnaturally fast and elusive he was.

So Don just stood there, frozen, as Max inched closer, looking down at him.

Suddenly, there was movement, and in some sort of detached way, it took Don a moment to realize it was *him*. He was attacking Max, this monster of a man who belonged to some sort of secretive "organization," quite possibly a clandestine alphabet agency. Don hadn't been in a fight since middle school, and yet his fist was in motion, going straight toward Max's chest.

The punch was wild, as if driven by a manic, desperate energy. Max swatted it away like a pesky fly, and in the same motion, he grasped Don's wrist, torquing it hard.

Don stumbled back, dazed, and attempted a kick. His foot stopped halfway to its target. *Stopped*. Max had simply reached out and grabbed it, and he'd done this so quickly that Don hadn't even seen it happen. With another unbothered motion, Max tossed him aside. Don smashed into the asphalt, rolling twice.

He moaned. Pain shot up his ribs and into his chest.

Groaning, he planted a hand on either side of himself, but before he could stand, Max was already upon him. Still Max's face was blank, but his eyes burned with a cold determination. Don felt a quiver in the pit of his stomach.

Don looked up at Max, defeated. He had no chance of winning in a fight against him, and he knew it. All he could do was lay there in a heap and wait for whatever fate Max had in store for him.

Max didn't attack, though. Instead, he spoke in that growling voice.

"Need your help," he said.

The tension in Don's balled-up body eased, and he turned his face to look up at Max, who now stood directly over him, looking down upon him, no signs of aggression. A moment passed, and Max offered his hand. Don took it, and the larger man effortlessly pulled him to his feet.

"Don't you want..." Max said and swallowed. "To help your friend?"

Kendall's face flashed through Don's mind. That smile. She smiled as much with her sparkling eyes as she did with her lips. It had been so long since Don had seen her.

"Of course," Don said. "But, man, I'm telling you, I'm in a bad spot. It's hard to help someone else when I can't even help myself, and—"

"How about this?" Max said and swallowed. "Help me, or I turn you..." He swallowed. "Over to your creditors."

Don's mouth gaped.

And for a moment there, he'd been thinking Max was a nice guy...

"You serious?"

Max nodded.

"And you don't want to test..." He swallowed. "My organization."

Don certainly believed him about that.

Shit...

Was this actually happening?

Don just stared.

"You ... you're blackmailing me?" he spat.

Max shrugged. "Call it what you will," he replied coolly and swallowed. "Do we have agreement?"

Don thought about the bind he was in. And he thought again about Kendall. Don was a firm believer in the notion that before a person can help others, a person must get one's own life in order.

But maybe he could help both himself *and* Kendall.

When the offer had come from a guy like Max and his organization, what choice did he have, anyway?

Don nodded.

"Good," Max said. "Come on."

He gave an encouraging swipe of the hand, then started down the alley.

For a moment, Don was rooted in place. Then he followed.

"Where are we going?" he said as he rushed to catch up.

Max didn't turn as he replied, "To the top dog."

"The mayor's office?"

Max shook his head. "Demetrio Toscani."

After everything he'd been through during the last half hour, Don's heart pounded faster than it had yet.

"*What?* Wait! Stop! Let's talk about this. Max, stop!"

Max didn't stop.

CHAPTER ELEVEN

KENDALL ANSON CLOSED her eyes and tried to ignore what was happening, though she was keenly aware of every thrust against her torso, every sound the man made as he moved over her, into her.

Just a few inches above Kendall's face, Ian Dalton's breathing was labored and ragged, and his fingertips dug into her skin. Hot sweat dripped all over Kendall, like rain—on her neck, her stomach, her breasts, her face. She smelled the filthy bedding and the musky scent of Ian's body.

Kendall wanted it to be over, but time kept stretching on and on, a seemingly endless ordeal. Some primordial instinct inside her thought of escape, of running away, of anything other than what was happening.

And for a moment, it seemed she *had* slipped away, found a space somewhere in the back of her mind that was blank and bright, a place of nothingness where she could dwell for a few moments. But then a sharp pain brought her back. Dalton was twisting one of her nipples hard.

He did that a lot. He liked to watch her squirm.

She yelped, then cried out, "Stop!"

Dalton scowled at her, gave her nipple a final twist between his fingers—a non-verbal *Go to Hell*—but he complied, removing his hand and planting it as a fist into the mattress above her shoulder, beside her face.

The old bed frame squeaked louder as his thrusting intensified, and Kendall closed her eyes again. No matter how often she did this, she couldn't escape the shame. Selling her body. Her mother would be disgusted with her. Her mother had always found prostitutes disgusting.

And that's what Kendall had been engaging in for months —prostitution. For the longest time, she hadn't thought of her actions with that label attached to them, convincing herself otherwise, but quickly she realized that even though she was selling her body to only one person—not dozens or hundreds—that didn't change the fact that she was selling it.

But she always reminded herself why she was doing it, the two-pronged reasoning—her situation and Cooper.

She thought of Coop now.

A moment ago, she'd been jolted out of that safe, distant recess of her mind when Ian twisted her nipple, and she hadn't been able to find her way back. But now she found Coop, just a hazy image, an indistinct yet comforting presence.

Finally, after what felt like an eternity, Ian finished and collapsed onto the bed next to her. He breathed heavily, and Kendall felt his heart pounding against her arm.

Several long seconds passed, then Ian stood and looked down at her as he scratched aimlessly at the sweaty patch of hair on the center of his chest.

"Get started with the cleaning," he said.

He turned to the desk by the window, pulled out a drawer, and tossed some crumpled bills in her direction. They fluttered onto the mattress by her thigh, which glistened wet.

She picked up the bills and flattened them out—a pointless and somehow feeble effort. Two twenties. She glanced up at him.

"This is only forty..." she said.

Ian scoffed. "And?"

Kendall pulled the sheet over her torso, covering her breasts.

"But ... I..." she faltered.

Ian laughed again, louder, a true laugh this time, not just a scoff. "Ten bucks? Are you really *that* broke?"

She didn't reply, averted her eyes.

"Shit," Ian said, snickering. "You know I'll get you the other ten dollars. Jesus Christ."

He clomped past her, and she turned away, didn't want to see his naked form—the chest hair, the sheen of sweat, his pinked flesh, engorged anatomy.

...and that wicked face.

The thin bathroom door thudded shut behind her, and after a moment, Kendall heard the shower turn on.

She lay motionless, gathering her strength and courage, which took nearly a full minute. Then she slipped out of the knot of sheets and blankets and began locating her items from among the clothes scattered on the matted carpet.

She slid into her panties, fastened her bra. Jeans next, then her T-shirt. She gathered the two twenty-dollar bills from the bed, stuffed them into her pocket.

And then she went to work. A rag waited for her on the desktop. For as meager and worn-down as Ian's possessions were, he liked to keep everything clean. His trailer was spotless. As she started wiping nonexistent dust from the desk drawers, she supposed she should be thankful for Ian Dalton's duel infatuations—cleanliness and sex.

Without them, Kendall wasn't sure what she would do. She was dependent on these fifty-dollar supplements to her meager income.

Her mind flashed to Ian's derisive laughter when she'd pointed out the missing ten dollars.

Ten dollars *was* an important amount of money to her. She needed every single dollar.

Everything tingled and ached from the moments-earlier encounter. She was used to Ian's roughness—the nipple-squeezing, hair-pulling, the violent thrusts. All of it served to further solidify in Kendall's mind that she was really in over her head, that she was giving herself away for money.

She thought of her mother again.

Yes, Mom would be disgusted with her.

As Kendall worked, she noticed a piece of paper on the floor that had fallen behind the desk chair. It was a hand-written note, folded in half, with strange markings scrawled on it. She picked it up, peeked under the fold.

It felt odd in her hands—foreign and out of place—because she was being sneaky. She didn't know what had come over her, choosing to grab this piece of paper that belonged to Ian. And the more times she glanced up to check if the bathroom door was still shut, the more it solidified her feeling that she was doing something wrong.

But she was going to do it, anyway. Bizarre curiosity had grabbed her in a stranglehold, and Ian had been treating her particularly poorly lately. It was okay to examine the note. For just a few moments.

She unfolded it. On it, in what seemed to be Ian's hand-writing, was a series of symbols. Three rows of three. Stars and triangles and squares in different configurations.

She heard the squeak of the shower faucet. The sound of the shower ceased. She folded the paper in half again and put it back where she'd found it behind the chair, angling it just as it had been.

A few minutes later, she'd finished the bedroom cleaning and was now in the living room. From the back of the home, she heard the bathroom door open. When she glanced back, she saw Ian walk past the doorway, naked again, sopping hair, slapping a towel across his back.

She began wiping the TV screen. As she did, she couldn't help but think about that mysterious note—and wondered what secrets it held...

CHAPTER TWELVE

DON WAS SOMEWHERE he never thought he would visit—Demetrio Toscani's mansion.

The home stood tall and imposing, framed by distant mountains and perched on a hill a block away, its white and grey facade giving the impression that it spanned for miles. Heavy velvet curtains adorned the windows. Ivy traced up impressive columns. A lengthy drive led to the entrance, and at the base of this drive was a guard station, where two stern guards stared toward Don and Max as they approached.

Don was a half step behind Max, who moved with quick, sure strides of his long legs. In a way, Max looked right at home in the midst of all the luxury—with his dark gray pants, sport coat, Italian loafers, Versace shades.

Don wore a sport coat as well. It was the final vestige of his previous life, just a tiny bit of nothingness he could cling to. He'd been wearing it for months. It smelled bad, and the wear-and-tear had gotten beyond just noticeable—it was atrocious.

But it was a sport coat. It made Don feel like he was still a gambler. And he wasn't going to let it go.

Aside from the jacket, however, he wore jeans, a soiled T-shirt, and worn-out sneakers. Underneath was a pair of boxers that he'd been wearing for more than two days.

Not that long ago, he didn't dress so very differently than Max, back when Don was a cherished high-roller at the casinos. The *real* casinos. Back in the days before he'd gotten greedy, turned to the seedier side of gambling.

Now, Don was just thankful to have shoes at all, something other than the work boots he wore during his ever more seldom landscaping shifts. He appreciated the ratty sneakers. At least they were comfortable. And he sure as hell appreciated the sport coat.

Desperation makes you appreciate things.

Despite the new sense of gratitude Don had been gifted via his recent struggles, it didn't change the fact that he looked like a bum as he approached the mansion.

More importantly, Toscani's mansion was somewhere he *never* should have gone, whether he was dressed well or not. A sensation of dread twisted Don's stomach, and he had to fight the urge to turn and run. He was in this position because he'd agreed to follow Max—this blunt, brooding stranger. As a Reno outsider, Max surely must not have understood the genuine danger that Demetrio Toscani posed.

Indeed, Max seemed unaffected by the atmosphere, walking steadily towards the two hulking, suited figures in sunglasses standing guard at the entrance.

"How know Kendall?" Max said without turning as they drew closer to the mansion.

Don took a moment with his broken English. "You mean, how do I know Kendall?"

Max nodded.

Don sighed heavily. "I met her a little over a year ago when I started at Garcia Landscaping. She was already working there. We had the same shift supervisor, Ian Dalton.

We hit it off and became fast friends. I'm nearly twenty years older than her, so the friendship has a big brother quality to it, though things did get a bit more complicated once. A coworker's barbecue. We'd both had a few beers. Ended up making out."

He hesitated for a moment, then continued. "I'm sure that must sound immature, a middle-aged guy telling you he made out with a chick at a party, but it was more than that. I've always felt something for her. From day one. She's something special."

He pulled his wallet from his pocket, took out the photo, handed it to Max.

"It's not like I've always carried that around with me!" he said, defending against any criticalness on Max's part. "Only since she drifted away a few weeks ago."

As Max studied the photo, Don looked at it, too.

A crease ran horizontally across the center; Don had to fold it to make it fit in his wallet. It was battered, and the edges were marred, but the subject was perfect.

Kendall's flawless, medium-toned skin was a canvas for her captivating brown eyes, almond-shaped with thick lashes. Her dark, straight hair fell in gentle waves around her face, accentuating her cheeks, lips, those eyes. Her smile radiated warmth and serenity.

"Beautiful, isn't she?"

Max nodded.

"Why'd she leave?" he said as he handed the photo back.

"She's not gone. She's just working very few hours at Garcia these days, and Dalton never schedules us at the same time."

"You don't talk..." Max said and swallowed. "On phone?"

"She stopped calling."

Max finally turned to him, arched an eyebrow over the top of his sunglasses.

"It's ... complicated," Don said.

Max nodded and left it at that, returning his attention to the immaculate sidewalk ahead of them. Toscani's mansion loomed larger as they approached. So did the guard station. So did the two guards staring them down.

"Kendall's originally from Arizona," Don said. "She's half white, half Native American."

Don paused, gathering his composure to go forward with the most sensitive part.

"And she's in a tough situation financially—she can barely afford her rental house now that Cooper got cancer and she has his medical bills. Oh, that's her dog. Cooper. Ol' Coop." He smiled. "Kendall's a bit of a loner, and she loves that dog more than life itself. But now she can't find a cheaper place to rent since most places require verifiable income and her second income is under-the-table cash. That's her second job outside of Garcia, another job with Ian Dalton."

"What kind of job?"

"That's .... also complicated. And it's the reason she hasn't called—she's ashamed of the work, so she won't speak to me."

Don left that last bit of information incredibly vague, but once again, Max said nothing. It was clear that Max had catalogued everything Don said, but he also knew when to let things breathe. This guy had diplomacy skills. Don could learn from him.

Maybe skills like those could help Don get out of his spot with the creditors...

"Today I've been thinking about her more than usual," Don said. "It would be a big day for her if she had more money."

"How so?"

"There's an animal charity event tonight at the Starlight Chalice downtown. She loves all animals, not just Cooper. The Nevada Friends of Animals always pairs its charity night with the Great Reno Balloon Race. It's this major huge hot air balloon event. An annual week-end-long thing. A big deal for the city. So the charity runs a casino night, and those who don't want to gamble can go to the roof and watch the balloon glow—that's when they light up the balloons but don't launch them. It happens at dusk. All those bright colors lit up. It's cool."

For a brief moment, Don swelled with pride for his city.

Max nodded.

They were almost to the mansion now, and as they drew closer to the guards, Don saw suspicious expressions on the men's faces. They rose from their chairs.

Max stepped forward. "Would like to go inside."

First, the two guards were shocked by Max's awful voice. After the momentary bewilderment passed, they exchanged a knowing look before the larger one, who seemed to be the leader, took a step closer.

His face was muscular and classically Italian with a dark beard, deep-set and close-set eyes, and a sloping brow marred by a striking scar over one of his eyebrows. He exuded a menacing presence.

"Got an appointment?" His voice was gruff and commanding, but it paled compared to Max's. This made Don feel a bit more secure.

Max shook his head.

"Then what do you want?"

"To speak with Toscani," Max said.

The guards looked at each other again—then burst out laughing.

Amid their mirth, Don saw a sudden flash of movement.

Max had punched one of the guards, the big one with the eyebrow scar.

In the goddamn throat!

The man's arms went to his neck, and he fell to his knees, gasping, spitting, coughing.

The other one's face went red with fury over his partner's throat punch, and he lunged at Max. The two massive men collided with a primal, earthy *thwack*.

Don watched as long limbs intertwined, pushing and shoving each other with unrestrained aggression, the sort of pure violence that arrests the senses of a bystander. It was like a dance, one partner pushing off the other. Both of their faces contorted with rage as they pushed and punched, neither one willing to budge an inch.

But within seconds, what had seemed like an even match shifted in Max's favor. He landed a punch that sent a dazed look flashing across the guard's face, and in that brief moment, Max grabbed the other man's arm.

Clearly, Max could handle the guy.

But how big of a pussy would Don be if he just stood there and watched? If there was one good thing about his current station in life, it was that it gave him a chance to make up for years of shortcomings.

So for the second time in an hour, and for the second time since middle school, Don Judkins was going to fight...

Filled with adrenaline and a bizarre sense of optimism, Don dove into the fray, recklessly targeting the guard's midsection with a wild punch.

The guard simply brushed him off—quite literally.

With a swipe of his massive arm, the man sent Don flying to the side.

Tumbling first on the concrete sidewalk, then the grass, Don rolled to a stop and looked up to see Max unleash a swift uppercut, sending the guard crashing to the ground in a motionless heap.

The other guard finally stumbled back to his feet, hunched over, one hand on his knee and the other clenching his throat. He glared at Max and Don with hatred in his eyes. As Max stepped past him, he reached out feebly, all his energy zapped, and quickly returned his hand to his knee.

"Toscani won't be pleased," the man wheezed.

Max ignored him as he went into the guard station and looked down at a control panel, which had a speaker and a series of buttons. He squinted in concentration for a moment, eyes roaming over the controls, then he reached out, and was about to press a big red button in the center, when a voice suddenly burst out of the speaker, bringing Max's hand to a stop halfway to the panel.

"Don't bother," an old Italian voice said. "Welcome to my home."

A loud *click*.

A loud *buzz*.

And the gate behind them began to retract.

Max looked at Don, then to the conscious guard—still with one hand on his knee and his other on his throat, still scowling. Max shrugged at the man, and a tiny bit of boastful pride showed through the stoicism of his stony face.

Then he turned, and with that determination with which he'd approached the guards, he headed up the drive toward Demetrio Toscani's mansion.

Don chased after him.

CHAPTER THIRTEEN

DALTON WAITED AT CITY PLAZA, an open space of walking paths and landscaping and outdoor art installations with steps that led down to the Truckee River. This was downtown, and everywhere he looked, he could see the city alive with activity —casino towers and shop fronts and traffic. People bustled about their day, and the sun blazed brightly over everything.

He glanced ahead and saw the famous Reno Arch spanning the street among the towers. It proclaimed *RENO: THE BIGGEST LITTLE CITY IN THE WORLD* in thousands of bulbs that, in a few hours, would shine brightly against the nighttime sky along with the rest of the area's over-the-top artificial luminance.

Dalton felt a strange energy pulsing through him, almost as if the city itself were calling his name. To Dalton, the downtown area was the most reminiscent of L.A., so it reminded him of his purpose, his need to push forward with the mission, even when faced with uncomfortable circumstances like the meeting he was about to have.

Also, seeing the smiling, well-to-do throngs of people

around him furthered his desire to chase his goal because it reminded him of how far he'd drifted away, how different he was from them now.

He glanced down, examined himself. He wore another Garcia Landscaping T-shirt, a pair of soiled jeans, and equally soiled work boots. Shit, he was so accustomed to dressing like this that he'd not even thought to clean himself up for this first face-to-face encounter with the partners.

As he glanced back up, his eyes fell on his vehicle, parked a half block away—his 1982 Chevy Citation. He'd gotten it just before he moved to Nevada, six years earlier, from L.A. It had already been a piece of shit before he left California, barely making the drive, and since then it had continued rotting away, piece by piece. The interior, with its cracked seats and stained dashboard, still smelled musty despite multiple attempts to get rid of the stench, and the light tan paint was riddled with decay.

It was as grimy as the clothing he wore.

He hated the car. And he hated that he hadn't been able to purchase anything better for years. There it sat. In the present moment. *Still*. It was still his. No matter the great strides he was accomplishing, no matter how important of a meeting he was about to hold with highly influential men, there sat the Citation.

Waiting to carry him back to his trailer.

Not to L.A.

To the trailer. In Reno.

Dalton looked away.

He'd been waiting for twenty minutes. Earlier, Boyd hadn't given a precise time when he and the partners would show, and anger was percolating as Dalton considered that perhaps Boyd was shunning him.

But then he saw three older men in suits approach the

corner. One of them was Boyd. Dalton straightened up and walked confidently over to them.

The partners watched him as he approached. All were in their seventies, all radiating wealth. Two of them wore blank expressions, while one—the fattest of them, the one with all-white hair—had a smug, condescending smile.

Dalton still couldn't believe it. They were actually showing themselves to him, revealing their faces, right there in the thick of downtown, beside the wide-open plaza, in the middle of the afternoon, broad daylight.

Still, although Dalton was now looking right at them, he only knew one of their names, the man he'd spoken to a few minutes earlier, the one on the far right.

Wallace Boyd.

Boyd was in his early sixties, probably the youngest of the three. He had a refined elegance and a time-forged sense of dignity, the sort of older dude who got shit done. Though Boyd worked in an entirely different field than Dalton's field of choice, Dalton had found himself emulating Boyd all the same. In another twenty years or so, Dalton *would* be like that man. Just like him.

Powerful. Rich. Respected.

"We're losing our faith in you, Dalton," the fat one said as they met at the corner.

"I know, and—"

"Word has it that police are beginning to tie the stabbings to the drugs," said the small, frail-looking one with liver-spotted skin. "Apparently, your man, Garrity, is gaining a reputation on the streets. How long will it be before people identify the Carver?"

"I've had a chat with Brooks Garrity," Dalton said. "He knows the price of his current actions."

The fat one spoke again. "Three months ago, our friend Boyd," he said, motioning to the man in question, "got word of a hungry up-and-comer. A shift manager at a landscaping company who sold pot on the side. A man who wanted to break out of a rut, to do better than his current lot in life, to run with the big boys, a man willing to do what is necessary for real power."

"I am!" Dalton shouted. Immediately, he recognized he'd been too enthusiastic, too anxious. In a calmer tone, he continued with, "And I—"

The fat one shook his head, spoke over him. "You convinced us you were the man with the resources and the know-how for our heroin operation. What you *didn't* tell us was that you'd be so sloppy."

Dalton held his hands up, palms out. "We're so close now to the final stage. You have my word that I'll take care of this. I can reign in Brooks Garrity. I swear it."

"And Boyd tells us you're concerned about symbols?" the liver-spotted one said. He had a raspy voice. "That you have Garrity out looking for markings on the syringes?"

"I don't know how you gentlemen acquired the syringes," Dalton said, addressing the three as a group, looking over them, "but they were either pre-owned or tampered with. Someone put a labeling system on them. It's nothing, I'm sure. But it's a way of keeping Garrity focused on the task."

The partners exchanged glances.

...which made Dalton even further suspect they knew more about the symbols than they'd let on. There *was* something to the symbols, and they weren't telling him.

"What do you know?" Dalton said quietly, letting his eyes roam over the trio again, ending on Boyd, the one with whom he'd been communicating, the one to which he had at least a modicum of understanding.

Boyd just stared back at him, eyes narrowing.

"You'd better hope you can control the Carver," Boyd

said. "For your own sake, Ian Dalton. We aren't men you want to cross."

The group turned and walked in the direction from which they'd arrived.

Dalton watched them leave.

CHAPTER FOURTEEN

DON STRUGGLED TO REMAIN COMPOSED, as though every nerve in his body was straining against his efforts.

He was sitting in Demetrio Toscani's office.

Max was beside him. That helped. But the presence of the two guards flanking Toscani's desk was heavy in the air. The one with the eyebrow scar glared at Max.

Don's heart pounded, beating a fearful cadence to the sense of impending danger that permeated the room. Toscani was a formidable spirit, even just the notion of him. He wasn't even there yet, and Don felt his limbs tense up.

Max dabbed a washcloth at a cut on his cheek. One of the guards had handed the cloth to him when he and Don had been ushered into the office, compliments of their unseen host. Don had always heard that Toscani was a class act. There might not have been any honor among thieves, but apparently notorious drug lords were hospitable.

The office was a modern art piece—black and white walls, with a hint of deep red and shiny glass accents. Its dark and intimidating aura of refined elegance reflected the personality of the man they were there to see. On one wall hung a large painting of a young woman dressed in a crimson dress, with a black mask that covered her eyes. On the other walls were a variety of old maps, some of which Don recognized to be of Reno itself. In the corner of the office stood a large stone statue of a man, its eyes closed, arms crossed.

The two guards were imposing figures. The one that Max punched in the throat continued to glower at Max, his neck still swollen and pink from the altercation outside. The other was a newcomer, but he was just as large as the one with the scar and the one that Max had left unconscious at the gate.

Demetrio Toscani finally breezed through the door with a measured gait. He wore a traditional Italian suit—charcoal gray with a maroon pocket square, accented with a few touches of gold jewelry—and he had a look of unyielding confidence on his face. He stood just under six feet tall with broad shoulders and a lean, muscled build that belied his age. His white hair and beard were neatly trimmed.

He went to the other side of his desk, eyeing the two visitors skeptically. Don felt his anxiety rising with every passing second. He tried to keep his face impassive, but he could feel his body tensing in anticipation. When Toscani's eyes took a moment to study Don, they bore into him.

Don swallowed hard.

Toscani took a seat behind the desk, a hand going to his face, where it cradled his strong, bearded chin. Don and Max were in the two chairs that faced the desk, and for a moment everyone stared at each other, two forces looking across an invisible demarcation line—Don and Max on one side; Toscani and the guards on the other.

Finally, Toscani spoke. "So, you two come to my home, accost my security personnel, and now you want information out of me?"

"Correct," Max said, zero hesitation.

Don tensed.

Toscani raised his eyebrows at Max's ruined voice. Then he scoffed, a deep, hearty laugh that matched his voice. "You two have balls. I'll give you that. But I fail to see how speaking with you will be of benefit to me."

Max leaned forward. "The guy we're after..." he said and swallowed. "Is killing your customers..." Another swallow. "And cramping your style."

"You're looking for the Carver."

Max nodded.

Toscani's grin brightened. "I thought that might be what this is about. Yet you come into Demetrio Toscani's office, and you *don't* ask him about the heroin deaths. You think it's someone else?"

Max nodded.

"You're possibly the only two people who think so." He paused. "And you're correct." Another pause as he scratched at his beard. "Who are you?"

"Max."

Toscani turned his gaze on Don. "And you?"

"I ... I'm Don Judkins."

Toscani's expression was even more surprised than when he first heard Max's terrible voice. His mouth parted in a surprised smile, and he exchanged looks with both of his guards, who grunted with amusement.

"*You're* Donnie Judkins, huh? You have quite the reputation around town, especially in the last few months. You know, I have a few associates who would just *love* to talk to you."

"I'm ... sure you do, sir."

Don creeped away as far as he could in his leather chair.

Toscani gave him a long stare, then turned back to Max.

"Just Max?"

Max didn't respond.

Toscani leaned closer over his desktop. "You haven't

shown any credentials, and my boys," he continued, waving his hand to indicate the behemoths on either side of him, "found no ID on you. Fed? DEA?"

"Private contractor," Max said.

Don squirmed again. He certainly hadn't contracted Max. Quite the opposite. Max had *conscripted* Don. But if Toscani thought that Don had brought Max into this situation, then Don's position in the city just got a lot more perilous than it already was, if that was possible.

He tried to escape farther back into his chair. There was no more room.

"Whoever you are," Toscani continued to Max, "you're clearly on the side of good, and it's eating you up inside to be in the office of an infamous drug lord, asking for assistance. I can see that in your eyes, big man. But don't forget—I've tangled with all types of do-gooders, including the DEA, FBI. And I'm still here."

Max didn't respond.

Toscani smiled then and eased back into his massive chair, lightening the tension in the room. "You said the Carver is 'cramping my style.' So you believe the Carver is tied to the ODs?"

Max nodded.

Toscani steepled his fingers and looked at the ceiling. "Yes, I've thought the same thing from the very beginning. Rumor has it the cops are finally starting to agree." He scoffed. "Idiots. They've not realized that all the killer drugs came with symbols. See, we found..."

He trailed off.

Because Max was reaching into his sport coat. He took out his vanilla-ice-cream notebook, took out the page with the pencil-scratching-revealed symbols, and reached it across the mahogany desk.

Toscani gave him a skeptical look, un-steepled his fingers, and took the paper.

"These symbols?" Max said.

Toscani nodded as he studied the paper. "Yes. But slightly different. There are a few variations."

Suddenly, he leaned forward again, looked at Max, flicking his eyes briefly in Don's direction. "So why in the world did you bring this dipshit with you?"

Max looked at Don, gave him an encouraging nod.

Don swallowed as he faced Toscani's intense stare. "I, um, know who distributed the killer drugs."

"Who?"

Don wasn't sure if he should answer. He hesitated, started to speak, but Max spoke over him, filling the void.

"Ian Dalton."

Toscani faced Max again. "Who the hell is that?"

"Just a guy," Max said and swallowed. "A landscaper."

Toscani laughed heartily. "Someone wanting to make a name for himself, yes?"

Max shrugged in an *It would appear so* sort of way.

"Interesting," Toscani said, then leaned back and looked away again in deep thought. A moment passed, then "Well, you're right. the Carver has been a concern." He paused. "But the drug issue is more critical for me. People are dying from that other shit that's flooded the market, and it makes my product look bad. My guys estimate a thirty-three percent drop year-over-year in *one month's time*. If it continues like this, it will be … calamitous for me. So if the Carver and the drug issue are the same, then that would simplify a potential solution."

He squinted at whatever he was looking at on the ceiling, going deeper into his thoughts. He turned back around, looking at Don first, then Max.

"But I know no more than you do. So exactly what information did you hope to gain by coming here?"

"The symbols. They must be..." Max said and swallowed. "The connection. You mentioned..." Another swallow. "Variations."

Toscani stared at Max, hesitating, weighing his options. He drummed his fingers on the desk and looked at them for a long moment. Behind his smile, his mind was debating something. Then he leaned back, pulled open a desk drawer and took out a piece of copy paper, handed it across the desk to Max.

Max took it and angled it toward Don so he could look, too.

Illustrations covered the page. They were similar to Max's, but not just the circle, square and triangle—there were several other markings.

"Yes, we've been tracking the symbols, too," Toscani said. "But we can't make sense of them."

He nodded toward the paper in Max's hands.

"Take it. It's a copy. Perhaps it will be helpful to you. And, now, what's helpful to you is helpful to me."

He gave Max a long stare, like his last statement had been some sort of informal union. *You scratch my back; I'll scratch yours.*

Max nodded.

Toscani's face relaxed fractionally, and he waved his hands. His sentries came off the walls and approached Don and Max. The man with the eyebrow scar stopped inches away from Max.

"Now get the hell out of my house," Toscani said.

———

As they walked down the street and away from the mansion, Don detected some sort of repressed frustration flashing across Max's countenance. Something was bubbling under the surface.

Whatever "organization" Max belonged to, clearly it was a righteous one, so it must have been burning Max to be in this situation—accepting the help of a known criminal boss.

They approached Max's Audi, which was parked along a side street. When they got to the car, Max pulled the folded piece of copy paper from his pocket and studied it.

Don leaned over. "Do the additional symbols help you?"

Max shook his head.

"If we could figure out the symbols," Don said, "we might be able to figure out the connection between the drugs and the Carver."

Max slowly lowered the sheet of paper. The narrowed concentration that had been on his face gave way to something like reluctance, almost defeat.

Odd...

Max sighed, and in a quieter version of his monstrous growl, he said, "I know someone who..." He swallowed. "Might crack the code..."

Don's eyes widened.

Why hadn't Max said anything about this already? That must explain why he'd looked so reluctant. Maybe it was a pride thing.

"Well, can you get the person here?" Don said. "Who is it?"

Max nodded.

"I can," he said and swallowed. "The person is an expert in—"

"Hey!"

A woman's voice called out from behind—urgently, almost frustrated.

Both Don and Max turned to look.

Halfway down the block, a beautiful redheaded woman was striding quickly, confidently in their direction. Sunglasses. Short hairstyle. Stylishly dressed. She looked like a model.

"You talkin' about me?" she called out.

CHAPTER FIFTEEN

DEMETRIO TOSCANI PUSHED through the door and stepped onto the flat, gravel-topped roof of his mansion. Arturo—his favorite guard, he of the massive arms and scar-sliced eyebrow—followed him. The sun was bright, and Toscani took a pair of sunglasses from his suit pocket, threw them on.

He should have been furious. The two men had come uninvited, managed to take down two of his top guards, including Arturo, and demanded an audience. But they had guts. Toscani admired that. And while he'd never been one to accommodate people's demands—let alone those of complete strangers—he'd also never faced something of this severity since he'd come to Reno, this double-threat of a new drug-pusher *and* the Carver. With both prongs of this attack, people were dying. Toscani hated that.

All those dead potential customers...

He went to the edge of the building, stopping just before the parapet. Arturo stepped beside him. Below, Toscani saw the two men a block away, standing by a maroon Audi.

Toscani had kept an eye on them as he crunched across the roof. When the men had gotten to the car, Max—the tall, dark, mysterious one sporting Hugo Boss—had pulled out the paper Toscani had given him and began studying it. The frumpy one, Ludkins, the one Toscani knew by reputation, stepped over and looked at the paper as well.

Even from a distance, Toscani could tell that Max was deep in concentration. Ludkins, too, was serious, asking questions that Max answered with a series of nods and shakes of his head. They had been giving careful analysis to the symbols that Toscani had given them, no doubt.

Toscani had seen only a moment of this, just as he approached the parapet, before a stunning redheaded woman had turned the corner in front of the Audi and approached the men, moving quickly, confidently, calling out to them. The men had stared at her as she approached, looking confused, momentarily arrested.

Max, particularly, appeared stunned. Toscani could read his bewilderment through his stony visage.

The woman continued to walk up to them, closing the gap. The men remained stationary, watching her approach.

By her clean-cut appearance and purposeful stride, she could very well be another professional like Max.

Apparently, Arturo had made a similar conclusion as he stepped closer to Toscani, ran a hand across his chin, and said, "This is trouble."

Toscani watched the trio for a few moments before he responded. The woman stopped when she was a few feet away from the men. No greetings were exchanged. They just stared at each other for a long, quiet moment.

"You might be right," Toscani replied to his guard.

"Do you trust them?"

"No, I don't," Toscani said as he narrowed his eyes, trying to make sense of the odd group gathered at the Audi. "That's why you're going to follow them."

CHAPTER SIXTEEN

RENO WAS ALIVE AND SULTRY, despite the sun's position still high in the sky. Everywhere Brooks looked, morons were howling hysterically in the streets, a few already staggering drunk. An overwhelming sense of revulsion surged through him as he analyzed these wretched people. This place was ghastly. What a dismal culture. What a dismal world.

Brooks stood to the side, leaning against a corner, looking into an alley, past a couple of utility poles, a dumpster, and to a battered metal door. He'd been there for forty-five minutes. The door hadn't opened.

But he wasn't panicking. He was using logic. Although his desire—that of wiping out as much of the modern contingent of disgusting humans as he could—came from an emotional place, the way he executed his ethical retribution was purely logical. And he was using this experience-forged logic once again to tackle this upcoming task.

This wouldn't be an idealistic kill like the others, however. This one was a necessity.

Finally, movement from the door. A woman exited into the alley.

Brooks immediately went into action, slipping into the space, using the angle of the wall to conceal his approach.

It was Calypso, the person he'd been stalking. She carried a black trash bag. Before the woman could reach the dumpster at the end of the alley, though, her gaze shifted for a moment—and she saw Brooks. Their eyes met. She quickly headed in the opposite direction at a run. She dropped the trash bag.

And Brooks bolted after her, allowing his primal instincts to take command. He sprinted, quickly making up the lost ground.

Closer.

Closer.

Calypso looked back over her shoulder right when Brooks was upon her. He tackled her from behind, sending her crashing down.

The impact of her body against the pavement knocked the wind out of her. She gasped desperately for breath, her eyes wide with fear and her limbs windmilling as she tried to escape.

Brooks took a firm grip of her arm. Furious with rage, he lunged forward with tremendous strength, the razor-sharp blade slicing through the air. Calypso released a deep cry as the knife pierced her abdomen.

He smacked a hand over her face and felt her hot tears against his palm, the vibrations of her screams, her gnashing lips and teeth.

Then it was over.

He removed his hand. Calypso's eyes stared vacantly into the sky.

Without hesitation, Brooks dragged her body behind the dumpster and looked up and down the alley for cameras. He saw none besides the one above Calypso's door.

Moments later, he was in the store, fumbling with the

security system. He located the tape and took it out of the deck, crushed it against the battered metal desktop, and for good measure, he put it in his pocket. He would trash it somewhere far away.

Brooks exhaled.

He'd avoided immediate disaster by eliminating Calypso, but he knew things would escalate soon. Everyone would hear about this. Everyone in the Reno underworld would soon learn that the notorious Calypso was the latest of the Carver's victims.

And if everyone heard about it, that meant *Dalton* would hear about it.

Brooks thought again about the ominous warnings Dalton had given him. This business with Calypso could prove disastrous for Brooks—unless he took measures to protect his reputation. He was going to have to do something preemptive. Something bold and decisive. A new course of action, something to show Ian how valuable a leader Brooks really was to their mission.

Brooks was going to do something drastic. He was going to shake things up. And he was going to do it today.

CHAPTER SEVENTEEN

"WELL, aren't you going to say hello?" Cerise Hillman said, loud enough to carry over the several-yard distance.

Her tone conveyed annoyance, which matched her feverish, almost angry steps as she marched up to Silence and Judkins.

Silence couldn't respond.

Of course, he was typically laconic, but at that moment, he was more than just quiet. He was utterly speechless.

Because there she was.

Cerise Hillman.

She wore tight, dark jeans, a red blouse, black mid-calf boots, Ray Bans. In her left hand was a black leather attaché case.

After Silence's meeting with Doc Hazel, he'd had a strong suspicion that his Specialist-therapist was going to make arrangements to bring Cerise into the assignment. She'd insinuated as much.

In that respect, it was no surprise that Cerise was there on the sidewalk in front of him, halfway down the block, moving rapidly, her figure flashing in and out of sunlight and pools of shadows created by the trees that lined street.

But in another, deeper way, Silence's senses were truly stunned.

There she was.

Cerise.

His mind flashed back to the memories, the same ones from Doc Hazel's hypnotherapy.

The pain at the side of his head and the face of the ugly pig of a man who'd brought the pain.

The flash of white.

Falling.

Cerise screaming, reaching for him. "Oh my God!"

When years have passed between encounters, there's always a moment of quiet reconciling when the brain is forced to align its memories with irrefutable new truths.

Silence was experiencing that phenomenon now.

It was Cerise's wavy, auburn hair that was throwing him for a loop. It was now at her shoulders, shorter than it had been two and a half years ago when it had been midway down her back.

As she drew nearer and crossed through another pool of sunlight, the details of her face flashed into clarity. Button nose, slightly upturned. Huge, almond shaped eyes.

Her natural beauty was blaring, forceful, and it looked like it had been plucked from the pages of history, only a few pages back, recent history. Her heart-shaped face and buxom figure looked like they should be painted on sheet metal beneath the cockpit of a World War II bomber, next to a line of victory marks.

Doc Hazel had said more memories could resurface, and at that moment, some of them did. But not specific memories. An amalgamation. A concept. That of the issues Cerise's beauty had presented in Spokane. She'd drawn stares. Everywhere they went. As with all of Silence's work, he'd needed to remain in the shadows. But Cerise had brought attention. Usually benign. But sometimes not—once, at least.

A restaurant. No, a bar. Had that been it? A bar? Silence sweeping over, cutting in, shoving a drunk to the floor. The guy had touched her. And Silence had touched him back. Hard.

A dust cloud had shot up when the man hit the floor.

So ... it couldn't have been a *floor*. It had to have been the earth. They must have been outside.

So where...

Silence halted his train of thought suddenly as panic swept over him. His mind had a tendency toward chaos, and during the years since C.C.'s death, he'd been able to manage it with the techniques she'd taught him—meditation, diaphragmatic breathing, mind-mapping, detachment.

But now his mind felt as chaotic as it had during the worst days of his previous life. He was tumbling, and he felt the sickening, dark sensation of instability closing in.

So he didn't use one of C.C.'s techniques. Instead, he went straight to the source.

He called out to her in his mind.

C.C., I need you.

Yes, love?

Is this—

Yes, this is actually happening.

Is that—

Yes, that's really her. Focus, love.

Silence took one of those deep, diaphragmatic breaths that he'd moments earlier rejected. He closed his eyes for a moment, watched the air's journey down into his lungs and back out his nose, then blinked back into the present.

"Max?"

It was Judkins. During the frenzied moment within his

mind, Silence had almost forgotten the other man was there. That was another reason Silence *had* to regain control of his thoughts: someone was depending on him.

He stood taller, recomposed, turned to Judkins.

"What's going on?" Judkins said.

"It's okay," Silence said and faced forward again as Cerise finally slowed down from her steady clip, stopping a few feet away from them.

She stared at Silence, as though waiting for a response. It took him a moment—as his mind had gone in a million different directions over the last few seconds—but he remembered that she'd shouted something from halfway down the block as she approached: *Well, aren't you going to say hello?*

"Well?" she said again, slightly out of breath but quieter than when she'd first called out.

"Cerise?" he replied. It sounded stupid. It *was* stupid.

"No, I'm just in your imagination."

She rolled her eyes.

"You're ... here," Silence said. It had come out instinctively, and just like his last statement, it was stupid.

Diaphragmatic-breathing wasn't a cure-all, apparently, because Silence sounded like a dope.

"I sure am," Cerise said, planting a fist on her hip. "That 'organization' of yours didn't give me much choice. I had to take time off from work for this. I hope you understand that. Had to travel across the country, too." Her eyes flicked to Judkins. "Who's your friend?"

Her concentration had ping-ponged. Like Silence, she had a mind that was easily pulled in different directions. He'd forgotten about that.

He'd forgotten so much about her.

And yet, seeing her now, he remembered her presence, which subsequently explained to him why he had been so hesitant to bring her onboard this assignment as a consultant.

Silence glanced at Judkins. The man bore a perplexed expression.

"Cerise Hillman, meet..." Silence said and swallowed. "Don Judkins."

Judkins offered Cerise a weak smile, and the two shook hands. Then Judkins brought his perplexed expression back to Silence.

"Max," he said, "what's going on?"

Before Silence could answer, Cerise cut in. "Max? Is that what you're calling yourself now?"

"Yes."

"So you were never—"

"No."

"That was, like, an alias?"

"Yes."

"Then, 'Max' is an alias, too?"

"Yes."

"So what the hell is your real name?" she said, louder, nearly shouting.

"Just ... just call me Max."

Judkins spun on him. "*What?* What is all of this? I'm supposed to trust you, man, and you didn't even give me your real name? And who is she?"

He pointed at Cerise.

Silence put a hand to his temple, rubbed, then exhaled a long sigh/groan. He felt teamed-up on, and as the leader of this newly formed motley crew, he had to get their focus back on the mission.

"She's our ... consultant," Silence said.

"A consultant! Max, I didn't—"

Silence held up a finger, cutting him off, and he looked at Cerise.

"I'm sure they told you..." he said and swallowed. "Why you're here."

Cerise gave another roll of the eyes. "Of course. But they were a little light on the details. Let me guess—you have some code you'd like me to identify, to translate?"

Silence nodded. He handed her the paper.

"Do you recognize this?"

Cerise's eyes roamed over the printout, and it was only a half moment before they widened with a sort of thrilled shock.

She looked up, met his gaze.

"Oh yes," she said. "I recognize these symbols."

CHAPTER EIGHTEEN

AN HOUR LATER.

Toscani was having one hell of a day.

He'd only just sat back down behind his desk—after his bizarre encounter with the mysterious Max and his washed-up gambler companion, Donald Judkins—when his intercom system rang.

He held a tumbler in one hand, a bourbon decanter in the other, just about to pour, and the two items remained frozen in mid-air, just as frozen as Toscani's face as he stared at the metal panel on his wall, the source of the buzzing.

Something about this seemed ominous, and a lazy, self-pitying part of him felt like ignoring it.

Instead, he placed the glass and the decanter on his desk, wheeled his chair a couple of feet to the side, and pressed the button.

"Yes?" he said.

Arturo's voice, scratchy through the speaker. Even with the distortion, Toscani detected hesitance in the man's tone.

"Um, sir, you have another insistent visitor. And, uh ... you're not going to believe who it is."

———

Toscani looked across his desk at the man facing him, sitting in the same chair that Max had sat in an hour earlier.

He looked just as the rumors had described him. Mid to late twenties. Dark blond hair, long strands, combed back. He wore a button-up shirt, and it was wrinkled, unkempt, like he'd seen some sort of action that day, a struggle, a scuffle. Average build. Pleasant face with a few nicks and scratches in a two-day beard.

On the surface, he was an agreeable-looking guy. But still Toscani found him repulsive. It was the eyes. The way he looked back at you. Toscani had existed among the criminal element for decades, so he easily recognized moral decay. And this guy had it bad. Even though the man was sitting in Toscani's office with the most congenial of expressions on his face, there was no hiding his eyes. The man was brimming with evil, eaten up with it.

"So here he is," Toscani said. "The Carver himself. The mystery killer that all of Reno is looking for. And you just decided to walk up to the home of the city's crime boss in the middle of the day and demand an audience?"

The Carver's faux-friendly facade cracked momentarily, revealing a sneer. "That's correct."

The guy wasn't physically imposing, but he was certainly unhinged. Those decades of experience in the criminal world that had leant Toscani the ability to recognize evil had also taught Toscani that the most threatening person in the room was the unhinged person—far more dangerous than the brash one or the muscle-bound one or the heavily armed one. The Carver appeared to have both qualities—evil *and* instability. This conversation was going to be a challenge; Toscani would have to plan his moves carefully. A twisted game of chess.

"What's your name?" Toscani said.

The man's facial muscles moved as he tensed his jaw. A moment of pause, and Toscani could see computations playing in the Carver's eyes as he weighed his options.

Finally, he said, "Brooks Garrity."

Toscani nodded slowly. "Normally when someone comes here without an appointment, I turn them away, Brooks, but this is the second time today that I've allowed someone in." He gave a dark chuckle. "We're all going through some strange times in Reno, so I suppose extraordinary times call for extraordinary measures. The men who visited me an hour ago—friends of yours?"

Brooks slowly shook his head, the dark expression remaining on his disarming face.

Strange...

"Then to what do I owe the honor of this meeting?" Toscani said. "I have a mysterious celebrity sitting across my desk from me, and I don't even know why."

"I'm not alone. I'm not a one-man team. The drugs. I work for the same man who released them."

Toscani exhaled.

Yes, he'd thought as much.

"You work for Ian Dalton," he said.

Though Brooks's dark expression didn't change, he tilted his head slightly, not able to conceal his surprise.

If there was any doubt that the man was being truthful, that he wasn't connected to the earlier visitors, it was erased now.

"Yes, I work for Dalton," Brooks said. His voice was cold and steady. "And I'm here to propose a joining of our forces."

Toscani played with this notion. He traced a finger on his desktop, giving himself a moment, then, "Why now? Those drugs have put a significant dent in my business for the last two months. Had we joined forces from the beginning, we might all be better off."

"Because it's time for Dalton's operations to expand," Brooks said. "And you hold all the power in the city. Better to cooperate than to compete. We know when we're beaten."

"You don't honestly think I'll work with him. You're out slicing people up." He scoffed. "I'm afraid that's just not a compelling business model."

Brooks held up his hands and offered a dark smile to go with his faux-defensiveness. "That's a personal matter, something that Dalton lets me indulge myself in. I've already told him I can stop, and I can certainly reign in my habits for someone as powerful as you, Mr. Toscani."

It was an effusive display of subservience. Over-the-top kowtowing. Still, Toscani admired the man's drive.

And he narrowed his eyes at the thought of it.

The new drugs had been killing people, yes, but by all accounts, they were highly addictive.

This could prove incredibly lucrative.

He looked Brooks right in the eye. "This might just be the merger I've been looking for."

CHAPTER NINETEEN

KENDALL'S BREATHING WAS CHOPPY, and her heart beat rapidly. She didn't know why she was doing this, why she was there.

She had the place to herself. She'd finished cleaning the entire trailer, and now she was preparing Ian's lunch. But she wasn't in the kitchen; she was back in Ian's bedroom, the first room she'd finished, over an hour ago.

Cleaning wasn't her reason for being back in the bedroom.

Her attention was on the desk, right there below her. It was by the window that looked out onto the lawn and the closest trailer, Ian's neighbor, Hal. She'd been told never to open any of the desk drawers. When it was time for her to clean the desk, she was to wipe the exterior. That was all.

Now, though, she stared at those drawers, and she felt the muscles in her arms ripple with anticipation.

It was sunny outside, bathing the desktop in bright light, casting crisp shadows from the stapler, the cup of pens, the box of paperclips.

She looked at the clock.

12:07

He'd said he'd be back at noon.

She was already pushing her luck.

A sound came from the other side of the trailer, and she jumped, thinking it was Ian, stealthily returning through the front door.

Immediately, however, rationality returned. The window was right in front of her, and though the curtains were closed, they were also sheer. She could see the gravel drive that traced the side of the trailer. The only vehicle was her Geo Metro. Ian's Citation wasn't there.

Just in front of the window were the drawers, beckoning her...

No, Ian wasn't home yet. The noise that had startled her had been the boiling pot on the stovetop; she was cooking Ian a pack of his knockoff Kraft Mac & Cheese.

The drawers continued to call to her—because she couldn't stop thinking about the bizarre symbols she'd found an hour ago when Ian had climbed off her and gone to the shower.

She already knew Ian was involved in heroin—and she was certain his were the tainted drugs people were ODing from around town, not Demetrio Toscani's—so the bizarre symbols seemed ominous to her. The intrigue had to be somehow connected to the threats plaguing Reno.

She could feel it. Ian Dalton was a wretched man. He was involved in the city's miseries. He *had* to be. And those symbols she found earlier must have been connected to it all somehow.

If she'd found the symbols on the floor by the desk...

...there were surely more *inside* the desk.

Another moment of hesitation.

The clocked ticked.

The pot rumbled in the distance, rattling the burner.

And Kendall reached for the desk.

She grabbed the center drawer handle, tugged it open. Pencils. Pens. Beer bottle caps. Chewing gum.

In the corner of the drawer was a stack of 3x5 cards. She grabbed the stack, thumbed through it like a flip book. Nothing. All blank.

She returned the stack, closed the drawer, opened another, one of the side drawers. There were invoices. Receipts. Shipping statements. Everything related to Ian's work at Garcia Landscaping. He was a shift manager, and she knew that he took a lot of his paperwork home with him, as he still had to do a considerable amount of physical labor during his shifts.

All the paperwork seemed legitimate, but she continued to remind herself of the bizarre symbols. Something was going on here. She knew it.

Then she saw a name written on a paper with a list of other names she didn't recognize. A nickname. One known as well to her as it was the rest of the Reno area.

The Carver.

She did a double-take, and a gasp parted her lips.

Beneath this note, were a series of other notes, the handwriting sloppy, as though they'd been jotted feverishly during a brainstorm.

I-90

Four distributions

Symbols?

TRAV HOTEL

The last note particularly stood out. The Trav Hotel? Even if Ian was involved in the killer drugs, why would he have that awful place written in his notes? The TV news shows had said that the Trav Hotel was one of the few places that hadn't been ravaged by the killer heroin. It was a conspicuous omission, given the place's reputation.

The notes were centered on the top page of a short, paper-clipped stack. Her fingers shaking, she flipped to the next page.

She found a series of listings. In kilograms. She remembered what her friend Don Judkins had told her when she started her bizarre partnership with Ian—that he suspected the man was involved in drugs. At the time, Kendall had known that Ian dealt pot, but she hadn't fathomed he would be involved in hard stuff.

Until he told her with his own lips.

It happened one afternoon in a post-furious-sex moment of transparency, spilling a few intimate thoughts with the woman with whom he'd just shared a grotesque excuse of an experience. He'd mused about the fact that Demetrio Toscani had too much power in the city. He said that he was graduating past pot, going to heroin.

Now, Kendall saw these kilogram notes on the pages below a sheet of paper that mentioned both the Carver and the Trav Hotel.

The implications of this combination were staggering.

Yes, her intuition had been correct. Something was happening here. If there indeed was a connection, what could—

Movement. Outside. She looked up and peered through the drapes. A car was crunching to a stop on the gravel drive.

Ian's Chevy Citation.

Shit! She'd gotten so engrossed in the mystery that she'd lost track of time.

From the kitchen, the rumble of the boiling pot of macaroni had gotten louder. She heard sizzling. It had overflowed.

She quickly rearranged the contents of the drawer as best she could and sprinted back through the trailer, coming to an awkward stop in front of the range. The water was boiling over the pot's rim, steaming on the burner.

Just as she turned the heat knob down with one hand and grabbed the spatula with her other, she heard the door squeal open behind her, followed by Ian's heavy footsteps. Fresh air wafted in, a cool blast drifting over the heat of the range. She didn't turn, just kept her attention on the food as she stirred.

"Lunch ready?" Ian said.

Kendall nodded without looking at him, eyes remaining on the food. "Just about. Mac and cheese. Ham sandwich."

Ian sniffed the air. "Smells burnt."

"The pot overflowed," she said and faced him finally.

Ian looked her up and down. "Why are you breathing hard?"

"I was in the bathroom when I heard it boil over. I had to run to get it," she said.

He just looked at her.

Then stomped past.

Kendall exhaled. When she heard the bedroom door shut, she made up her mind.

She would call her friend. Don Judkins. Someone she hadn't talked to for weeks. She'd been too mortified to speak with him since her encounters with Ian had gotten so ... intense.

She would have to be careful, though...

She craned her neck to the side and looked down the hall. The bedroom door was still closed.

Her purse was on the counter. She fished out her cellular phone, dialed the number by heart, and waited.

The call rang.

And rang...

Her fingers trembled.

Answer, Don, she thought, willing her friend to action. *Please, answer!*

CHAPTER TWENTY

A WHILE EARLIER, when he was downtown, Brooks had fought against sensations of revulsion at the decrepit society he was engulfed in.

But that was downtown.

This place was much, much worse.

The Trav Hotel had a long and storied history in the city of Reno. The hotel tower and the sprawling complex that surrounded it used to be called the Travis Hotel & Casino, a highly regarded and popular establishment. During its heyday, it was a vibrant hub of activity, hosting gamblers and celebrities alike. Many of the city's elite were frequent guests, and the hotel was a go-to spot for people looking for a luxurious getaway.

All of that changed two decades ago, when the business failed and the hotel was left abandoned and decaying. The homeless and vagrants soon moved in and transformed the place into a makeshift shelter. In time, it became an underground hub for drug handoffs, shady dealings, and all kinds of illicit activity.

The local police knew what was going on inside the hotel,

but there was little they could do about it, particularly after mob boss Demetrio Toscani took an interest in the place; many of his best clients frequented the Trav Hotel. Toscani's sphere of unofficial influence had protected the place for years until it turned into the rotten city-within-a-city that it was today.

The name itself, "Trav Hotel," was a testament to the establishment's tumultuous past. It was derived from the vandalized sign that hung above the entrance, which had been stripped of the *I-S* from *TRAVIS* and the *& CASINO* at the end of the title, leaving only *TRAV HOTEL*.

The name stuck.

The Trav Hotel. Or, simply, the Trav.

Brooks had already received innumerable looks from scumbags as he crossed through the crumbling concrete to the main five-story tower. He wore a baseball cap and had the collar of his jacket turned up, hiding as much of his Carver-identifying features as he could.

As he stepped through the main doorway where a set of revolving doors had once existed, the smell of decay and desperation filled his nostrils. He could feel the eyes of addicts and vagrants upon him. He heard wheezing and coughing. A man asked for a dollar. Despite his revulsion, Brooks reminded himself why he had to enter the Trav.

Trash and debris were strewn across the floor, and the walls were stained and crumbling. Rats squeaked and scratched from inside the walls. Further down the corridor, he could hear the moans and cries of addicted souls. The smells of stale beer, vomit, and sweat intermixed.

Brooks marched down the hallway, feeling the penetrating stares from those lurking in the shadows. The hollow resonance of the place was occasionally broken by muted laughter or a muffled whisper.

He rounded a corner, and there it was—Room 124. He

stole a glance back, ensuring his path was clear, before pushing open the door, which hung from a single hinge.

As he stepped into the room, he heard a low voice from somewhere behind him, "Don't say I didn't warn you."

Brooks spun around and saw an old man perched in a nearby doorway with a smirk on his face. He cackled. He looked drunk. Or high.

Turning his back on the man, Brooks resumed his mission, entering the space. Torn furniture. Broken and boarded walls. Cigarette burns in the scraps of remaining carpet. A pile of beer cans in the corner. Graffiti everywhere.

The floor squeaked under his feet as he continued inside. It was warped, the plywood surface buckling, stained with a mix of dirt, blood and God-knows-what.

He crossed through the filth. This had been some sort of suite, so first he checked the separate bedroom. Then the bathroom. They were just as ruined as everything else, but there was no one home.

Satisfied, he crossed back through the space to the kitchen. With no one in the suite, he could retrieve the item he'd stashed there two months earlier. He reached into the cabinet, fingers exploring the rot, and found the cigar box.

He opened it. Six syringes. Each with the symbols at the top. He studied them. The first five bore sets of symbols he'd already seen on drugs he'd distributed earlier during this endeavor.

A wave of cold panic sweat flushed his skin, but as he looked at the final syringe, he exhaled in relief.

There, at the top of the final barrel, was a different set of symbols, one he'd yet to see.

It included an octagon.

Brooks smiled. This was it. Now, even if he had made a colossal mistake by murdering Calypso, at least it had come with a happy ending. The ends justified the means.

Dalton would be ecstatic that Brooks had made a huge stride in deciphering the symbols. A small, satisfied laugh escaped his lips, as much joy as it was relief. He felt honest-to-God tears form in his eyes.

This would set everything right.

But he wouldn't tell Dalton that he'd joined forces with Demetrio Toscani. Not just yet.

He took out a notebook and copied down the sequence of symbols. Before he'd finished the note, there was a *clunk* behind him. He whipped around, dropping the box.

He'd checked the bedroom and the bathroom in the back of the suite, but what he noticed in that adrenaline-fueled frozen moment of panic was that he'd somehow not noticed a small door to the side of the suite's kitchen area where he now stood—it belonged to a half-bathroom.

The door swung open, and two men exited—one black, one white, both with dilated pupils, both wearing rags, both hulking.

They approached, sneering. Behind them, on the bathroom sink and floor and the rim of the bathtub, was a collection of drug paraphernalia.

"Didn't hear you knock," the taller one said.

The shorter one was also fatter and had a mustache. He looked Brooks up and down, just like all the other scumbags had since Brooks arrived at the Trav.

"Well, ain't you a clean-cut fella? You work for Toscani?" He had a nasally voice.

Brooks hated to give these degenerates the validation of a response, but he knew he was in a precarious situation. He summoned his acting abilities again, like he had so many times as the Carver. Time to transform. To radiate simpleness. Purity.

"Aw, jeez. I get caught for everything," he said with a smile, looking away guiltily. "I'm working on a college project.

About the drugs, ya know? I heard I could get some of the bad shit here. You guys want to be in a documentary?"

The men looked at each other. A brief pause. Then they burst out in laughter.

"A documentary? Fool, you trespassed into our home, and you're asking us for a favor?" the tall one said.

"We don't like intruders," his partner said and pulled a large knife from behind his back.

Brooks eyed the weapon.

The man's knife was larger than the one Brooks had brought, but Brooks could rightly assume he knew better how to wield a blade.

This wasn't a pissing match, after all.

He looked back up, met their sneering faces...

Then sprung at them.

Two long steps, and he was right on the fat one, grabbing the arm with the weapon. He twisted. The knife dropped, its point thunking into the filthy carpet.

Brooks lowered himself and used the man's bodyweight to flip him over his shoulder. The man landed on his back, cracking the flimsy floorboards.

Arms grabbed Brooks from behind. The taller guy. Brooks was in a full nelson. He rammed his head back into the man's face and used the moment while the man was stunned to pull himself out of his grasp. He ducked under the man's shoulder, pulling his hand with him as he went.

He now had the man's arm twisted behind his back. With one swift motion, Brooks flung the man over his extended leg, sending him into the refrigerator. His head *cracked* against the door. Skin split. Blood gushed out. He collapsed into a motionless lump.

He'd hit hard. Broken neck, most likely.

Brooks didn't hesitate. He spun back on the fat one.

The man put his hands up, looking absurd as he did so, bloodied and lying on the floor. Absolutely pathetic.

A look came across the man's face, a look of realization that overpowered his fear. "You're the Carver?"

Brooks grinned.

And answered the man's question.

He twirled the knife in his hand, letting the man see it, letting him *really* see it.

Then he plunged it into the man's sternum. The man had one last, desperate howl, then went silent.

Satisfaction washed over Brooks, a feeling of power. Just to be safe—and as a cherry on the top—he turned around and slit the throat of the unconscious man slumped against the refrigerator.

"Hey!" a voice shouted from behind.

The front door stood open. A man was there. It was the old guy who jeered at him before he'd entered the suite. Behind him were a half dozen other vagrants.

And they all stared at Brooks, knelt in front of a dead, slashed man.

Blood gushing down the man's neck, onto his shirt. Blood covering Brooks's knife and the hand holding it. Blood everywhere.

One of the vagrants screamed out, *It's the Carver!*

And another, *The Carver!*

In that moment, Brooks assumed they would scatter. But apparently there was some sort of derelict code of honor at the Trav Hotel.

Because, with rage on their faces, the entire group rushed into the suite.

Brooks sprinted off, going for the back patio.

CHAPTER TWENTY-ONE

DON USED one hand to clench down hard on the leather passenger seat as the Audi barreled down the highway, swerving through traffic. His eyes went wide, and he gripped tighter as he watched the tailgate of a much slower pickup truck come up to the windshield rapidly. At the last moment, the Audi swerved into the passenger lane and swept past the truck.

With his free hand, Don kept his cellular phone pressed to his ear.

"Okay, Kendall," he said. "The Trav. We're headed there now." He paused. "Did Dalton hurt you?"

Kendall didn't respond.

"Did he *hurt* you?" he repeated, instantly regretting his harsh tone. He wasn't angry at Kendall; he was *enraged* at Ian Dalton. Because he knew the answer to his question through his friend's tone.

She'd whispered the entire phone conversation, saying that she had to be fast, that Dalton was in the back of the trailer. She'd sounded on the verge of tears the entire time.

After a pause, Kendall's whisper came back, sounding urgent. "I gotta go!"

"Kendall!"

A shuffling sound. And the line went dead.

"Shit!" Don shouted. He collapsed his phone and put his newly free hand on the opposite side of his seat cushion. He turned to Max in the driver's seat.

Without taking his eyes off the road, the big man said, "How much farther?"

Kendall had called Don—for the first time in weeks—after he and Max and their new companion, Cerise Hillman, had converged outside Demetrio Toscani's. Cerise had just started looking over the symbols that Max had handed to her when Don's cellular phone rang.

Kendall had told him she found a note of Dalton's, one that was connected to his heroin dealings and mentioned the Trav Hotel. Don relayed the info to Max, telling his new partner about the Trav's notorious reputation and the fact that it had, as of yet, to be affected by the killer drugs. Max had immediately sent everyone to the vehicles and barreled off toward the Trav.

Now, Max reached into his jacket pocket and took out his cellular phone and his small notebook with the vanilla-ice-cream-esque plastic cover, into which the mysterious Cerise woman had written her phone number just before they took off. Still without taking his attention off the road, Max used his thumb and flipped through the pages, somehow blindly finding the exact page with the phone number Cerise had written.

"Call number," Max said and swallowed, shoving the phone and notebook in Don's direction. "Use speakerphone."

Don hesitated. While he wasn't a particularly contrary individual, he hadn't planned on Max giving him orders. He'd thought this would be more of a partnership, less of an internship.

He looked at the phone, then flashed his attention to the rearview mirror. A blue Dodge Spirit was right behind them, matching Max's urgent pace and maneuvers expertly. Cerise was behind the wheel.

"Who is this Cerise Hillman woman?" Don said.

"A cryptographer," Max said and swallowed. "DOD employee."

The Audi quieted slightly and slowed as a car pulled into the passing lane in front of them. A moment later, the car signaled and went back to the right, and Max gunned the gas again. Don's head whipped back with the momentum, and he scrambled to reaffirm his grip on the seat cushion.

Don shot a look in Max's direction. Max ignored him, steely eyes still locked forward.

"There was a weird vibe back there," Don said. "What, is Cerise like an ex-girlfriend or something?"

"I'm engaged," Max said immediately. There was a hint of defensiveness in the man's growling tone, something that felt strange, unwarranted.

Don was so puzzled by the response that for a moment he couldn't form his own response. Then he said, "I didn't ask if you were with her now; I asked if she was an *ex*-girlfriend."

Max didn't respond.

Not only was this guy mysterious and dark, but he was also perplexing.

"If we're going to work together on this," Don said, "if you're demanding my assistance, then I need to know what's going on."

Finally, Max acknowledged him, flicking his eyes in his direction for just a moment before looking at the highway again.

"She was in your position..." Max said and swallowed. "A

long time ago..." Another swallow. "I helped her like I'm helping you."

Did you also practically kidnap her like you've done with me? Don thought.

But instead of venting that frustration outwardly, he said, "A cryptographer. Then she's here to help with the symbols?"

Max nodded.

"So what was with the tension?" Don said.

Max didn't respond.

Don groaned. "Whatever."

He entered the phone number, pressed the green rubber *SEND* button, activated the speakerphone function as Max had requested, and placed the phone on the center console.

One ring, and Cerise answered. "Yes?"

Don checked the rearview again. Behind the wheel of the Spirit, Cerise now had a cellular phone pressed to her ear.

"What are the symbols?" Max said.

"It's not a logographic system," Cerise said. "It's much less sophisticated than that. Each symbol corresponds with a letter, maybe a number. It's some sort of homemade cipher. I'll need some time to sit down with it."

"Fine."

Max collapsed the phone, returned it to his pocket.

Realizing his attention had drifted away from his navigational duties, Don looked back to the highway just in time to see the green road sign coming up fast.

"There!" Don said, pointing through the windshield. "That's the exit!"

————

Aside from being the most notorious location in Reno, the Trav Hotel was one hell of an eyesore—all broken concrete and weeds and litter. Once a sign of opulence, it now housed many people with no other place to go. The homeless, drug users and other downtrodden souls gathered here in search of a safe haven.

The Audi rolled to a stop at the corner of the block. Max killed the engine, and he and Don both got out, heading toward Cerise's Spirit, parked just behind them. As they approached, Don heard the doors unlock. He followed Max's lead and climbed into the back seat.

Cerise locked them in. Don looked around. The car was spotless and had the new-car smell.

A brand-new vehicle. And parked in front of it, a fancy Audi. As a Reno local, Don knew this was *not* the way to roll up to the Trav Hotel.

Indeed, as Don glanced out the window at the crumbling five-story tower and its destroyed surroundings, he could already see lots of people staring in their direction. Anxiously. Like they would stroll over to start some sort of trouble at any moment.

Cerise turned around to face them in the gap between the two front seats, and Max reached forward, handing her the note they'd been looking at outside Toscani's before Don had gotten the call from Kendall.

"So you can…" he said and swallowed. "Decipher them?"

Cerise nodded. "Yes, but the three I've already broken are nonsense words. *Coffee, cat, apple*. Which means this must be a multi-layered system—symbols leading to words that are themselves some sort of cipher. The symbols are easy enough, but I'll need time to crack the cipher key."

Max nodded and shifted his weight back. The bench seat wheezed with his mass, and the cushion's displacement was so dramatic that Don felt it.

"Get started," Max said. "I'm going to visit…" He swallowed. "Hotel Trav."

He went for the door handle.

Past Max's shoulder, through the window, Don noticed someone he recognized sprinting out of the dilapidated building. He leaned forward, his eyes glued to the figure in the street.

"Oh my God..." Don said.

Max stopped, turned to him, then followed his sightline.

Don watched through the window as a figure burst out of the remains of a first-floor patio at the Trav Hotel's main tower. There was a serious look on the man's face, one of survival. He bolted forward—a baseball cap fluttering off his head—stumbling on a slab of concrete before darting off again, chased by a half dozen vagrants, who flooded out of the same door.

"It's Brooks Garrity!" he cried, pointing out the window. "I told you!"

Max and Cerise both turned to look.

"The man you suspected," Max said.

"Right. He works with me at Garcia Landscaping," Don said. "Another one of Ian Dalton's employees. Follows the guy around like a puppy."

Max whipped around on him.

"Dark blond hair. Five-foot-nine," Max said and swallowed. "Just like—"

Don nodded. "The descriptions of the Carver. But does that mean..."

Don couldn't finish his sentence.

Because Max had already bolted out of the car.

CHAPTER TWENTY-TWO

THE CHAIN-LINK FENCE screeched as Silence pushed through a gaping hole and sprinted across the barren urban landscape to the tower ahead, where the blond man was being chased by a handful of people who'd funneled out of the building. He watched as the guy took a turn back into the building through an open doorway with a battered steel door lying on the concrete beside him. His pursuers chased after him, and they all disappeared.

"Dammit!" Silence growled, sending pain through his throat.

He sensed the weight of the shoulder-holstered Beretta against his ribs as he sprinted up to the building, past another group of people in rags, these huddled around a portable radio, watching him in awe.

Silence sprinted into the tower and drew the Beretta. Before him stretched a hallway of wreckage with shattered furniture and a handful of homeless people lurking in the darkness. Suddenly, he saw a streak of movement and immediately reacted.

As he rounded the corner, he encountered the group of

people who had been on the heels of the blond-haired figure, all of them breathless and full of bewilderment.

Silence ran by them, then halted. He paused to listen and heard a noise farther ahead. Taking off again, he raced up a staircase in the dilapidated structure.

When he reached the second story, he saw the man sprinting down the corridor ahead of him.

There were sophisticated ways to feel out a situation. And then there were blunt ones.

Silence went with the latter.

"Carver!" he yelled out, which sent another pulse of pain through the scar tissue of his throat.

The guy instantly looked back over his shoulder, making eye contact, mouth falling open. He turned a corner.

He'd answered to the name Carver. There had been immediate recognition in his eyes. That was good enough for Silence. He tightened his grip on the Beretta and bolted after the man.

As he pushed around the corner, someone jumped out at him from the threshold of an empty elevator shaft.

Silence saw the glint of a knife just before the Carver lunged. Instinctively, he stepped back and caught the man's wrist, sending the blade clattering on the ground. The Carver was average-sized but wiry, and he fought hard against Silence's grip, pushing fiercely as he screamed out animalistic shrieks that echoed through the hallway.

Silence pivoted his weight into his hip, using the momentum to spin the Carver over, and he smashed the other man's face into the linoleum with a loud *thwack*. He shoved his Beretta into the man's temple and growled, "Stop! *Now!*"

The energy in the air shifted, and the Carver complied, all of his feral vigor slackening. With a final deep breath, Silence got to his feet, yanking the other man up by the shirt. He jabbed his gun into the Carver's lower back.

He looked around at all of those who had been watching them fight. There were four people in this stretch of hallway —two peeking out of doorways and two hunched on the floor. All were watching, frozen in place, terrified by what had just taken place.

And with a shove, Silence began marching his prisoner to the stairwell.

For weeks, the Carver had terrorized the city.

Now, he'd been captured.

CHAPTER TWENTY-THREE

KENDALL STOOD THERE IN PANIC, her mind a jumble of thoughts. She'd been in a mad rush to leave Ian's trailer, but now she was frozen in place.

Because she couldn't find her damn keys.

Shit, of all the times to misplace them!

She tore through the contents of her purse. Gum. Tissues. A wadded-up receipt.

Then she realized...

Her purse felt lighter than usual. Something else was missing, something that had a bit of weight to it.

Her cellular phone.

Had she—

A voice made her jump. "Missing these?"

It was Ian, leaving the bedroom, approaching from the tiny hallway. He held up Kendall's keys and her phone, then raised his other hand and waved a small flap of clear plastic tape.

"I told you to never open my desk," he said.

She gasped, her chest rising and lowering rapidly.

"Just a small strip of tape," Ian continued, giving the tape in his hands a shake. "That's all you need. A rudimentary security system. Place it over a crack, and if you come back to find it torn, you know someone has opened the door you placed it on. Or, in this case, a drawer."

He paused.

"I put a strip of tape on each of my desk drawers, Kendall. Don't take this personally, but I haven't fully trusted you for some time. Looks like those instincts of mine were onto something."

He kept coming toward her. He was only a few feet away.

"This tape was torn. You've been in my desk. What were you doing there?"

Fear coursed through Kendall's veins, an electric pulse. She was a cornered animal, her heart thudding in her chest, unable to move or speak. She held her breath, bracing for anything.

"Why were you snooping around? What did you find?" Ian snarled.

He was livid, his brow furrowed in rage. A vein protruded from his temple.

He gave her a moment.

And when she didn't answer, he shot forward and grabbed her throat.

She gasped for breath as his fingers tightened around her neck. She swiped at him, but quickly her vision lightened, and a cool sensation swept over her skin. Her body went rigid, her breath coming in shallow gasps.

Relief flooded through her as air rushed into her throat. He'd released her neck, throwing her to the side. She smashed into the wall, and pain swept over her.

Ian reeled back, and with a single, swift movement, he backhanded her face.

The force of the blow sent her crashing to the floor.

Agony washed over her body like something tangible, like a rolling wave.

Quickly, that pain was eclipsed by a new pain. Then more. There was so much pain that it all cancelled itself out as Ian's fists pummeled her back. He screamed at her, incoherent. She was screaming too, as agony surged through her body, coming like explosions.

Her vision faded. The pain was unbearable, and she felt her consciousness slipping away. She nearly succumbed to the darkness, her body limp and broken, when...

... there was a knock at the door.

The impacts stopped. Her agony coalesced in that moment of reprieve, throbbing as a singular force, one giant pulse.

Panting, Ian just looked at the door for a moment before he gruffly exclaimed, "Yes?"

A friendly but concerned voice with a folksy twang called out. "Everything all right?"

Kendall recognized the voice. It was Hal, Ian's next-door neighbor.

"Shit..." Ian muttered under his breath. Then he shouted back at the door, "It's all good, Hal. Go home."

Hal responded immediately, and when he did, his voice was stern. The guy had a kind heart, but he was no weakling. Far from it.

"Open the damn door, Dalton," Hal said. "I heard screaming."

Ian looked down at Kendall. They locked eyes. He was full of fire, his face flushed, covered in sweat.

A moment passed, and he bounded over to the door, threw it open, pointed at Kendall.

"Is *that* what you heard, Hal?" he shouted. "That slut?"

Hal's mouth opened. "You son of a bitch..."

He was a big guy with a big face and a big beard. Flannel

shirt. Torn jeans. The kind of guy who'd help change your flat tire, then buy you a beer since you'd had such a shitty day.

And he could have been Kendall's way out of this, but she needed to act quicker, immediately, zero delay. She also knew the longer Hal was involved, the more danger the man was in, because she now recognized that Ian was an even more dangerous individual than she'd thought.

Deadly.

So Kendall used the moment to snatch her keys and cell-phone from the carpet where Ian dropped them, hop to her feet, and rush out of the trailer.

Hal called after her, "Ma'am, wait!"

But Kendall was already inside her Geo.

She turned the key, threw it in reverse, and took off.

CHAPTER TWENTY-FOUR

SILENCE SHOVED the Carver through the urban wasteland, away from the broken and wretched Trav Hotel.

For weeks, Reno had been on the lookout for the Carver. Someone had to capture the serial killer who had been terrorizing the city.

It might as well be Silence.

But Silence wasn't a lawman; he was an assassin. He was accustomed to assassinating.

Every inch of him wanted to have already eliminated the piece of shit, to have left a corpse with two bullet holes in its forehead back there in the decrepit building—either for the vagrants to discover, or to rot away with the sands of time.

That's not always how things turned out, though. Silence was one of the Watchers' weapons, yes, but he wasn't just a blunt instrument, and the Watchers weren't simply mad executioners. Typically, there were problems to be fixed, intel to be gathered, mysteries to be solved.

And before Silence could end this man—this "Brooks Garrity," as he now knew his name to be—he had to find out what Garrity knew about the deadly heroin, the symbols on

the syringes, and the connection between Ian Dalton and
mob boss Demetrio Toscani.

Silence was sweaty and grimy from the scuffle. So, too,
was Garrity, though he was much worse for the wear. Their
shoes crunched through the ruined terrain. The air was thick
with dust and cigarette smoke and marijuana. Sirens droned
in the distance.

Silence walked right behind Garrity, his Beretta shoved in
the man's lower back. He was using his sport coat to conceal
it, but this was a lackluster effort—as he had to walk only
inches behind the other man—and they drew stares from the
camps of homeless people they passed.

Many of the people put the pieces together—this five-
foot-nine, sandy-blond-haired, beaten white guy being
marched by a man in dress-casual clothes, sticking a gun in
the first man's back.

They whispered.

It's the Carver!

Holy shit, they caught him...

Halfway through the open lot, as they drew nearer to the
Audi and the Spirit, Silence could make out Cerise and
Judkins watching them approach through the Spirit's
windows. He saw their lips move in an animated
conversation.

Garrity had said nothing since he was captured. Silence
wasn't much of a talker, either, but he needed to get intel out
of this piece of shit. And fast.

So, as they pushed forward, he gave the Beretta a quick
jab into the other man's back and said, "Talk."

Garrity gave a sinister chuckle. "Talk, huh? Want to know
why I've done these awful, awful things, why I stabbed so
many sweet, innocent people?"

Silence didn't respond.

"Everywhere I look, I see sin, filth, debauchery, and every fiber of my being is sickened. I see it in the fools who throw away their hard-earned money in casinos and bars, or in their ignorant subservience to mind-numbing advertising. I see it when they stuff their ugly faces with shit food. Drunks. Hookers. Potheads. Perverts. They're everywhere. And unless more people like me do something about it, their numbers are going to grow."

For a brief moment, Silence considered a similarity—his position as a Watchers Asset, an assassin paid to kill society's worst-of-the-worst.

His conscripted mission wasn't so different from Garrity's self-prescribed one.

Garrity looked back at Silence as he finished his wicked speech. Grinning. His eyes were dark. His face dripped with sweat. To most people, it would have been an unsettling visage. Silence was unaffected.

"You work for Ian Dalton," Silence said.

Garrity shrugged and turned his attention forward again before replying. "True. But just today, I accepted another exciting business opportunity."

Silence frowned. "What does that mean?"

Before he could get an answer, Garrity let out a piercing wolf whistle. A group of men materialized from the ruins. Three of them. Coming from different directions, closing in a half circle around Silence and Garrity.

Silence stopped.

The men were sharply dressed, unlike the vagrants and drug addicts that populated the area.

Garrity looked back at Silence again, and this time he came to a halt, turning all the way around to face him. The dark grin on his lips grew wider.

"You didn't think I'd go to the Trav without backup, did you? Meet my new work pals." He gestured at the well-dressed men, who were slowly approaching. "I joined up with Mr. Demetrio Toscani, just this very afternoon."

They were all large men. Wearing Italian suits. Though their hands were empty, Silence saw the slight bulge of shoulder holsters beneath their jackets.

They wouldn't pull out their weapons. Not here. Not in this busy, infamous location.

Not unless Silence did something brash. If he did, they'd cut him down in *Godfather*-tollbooth-ambush style.

One of them gave a little chin lift toward Silence and paired it with a smirk. Silence took the meaning.

He lowered his Beretta.

As Garrity began walking backward toward the other men —flashing that evil grin—Silence felt a flash of anger and frustration.

He'd caught the bastard.

He'd had him.

He'd been looking forward to eliminating him.

And now he had to let him go. A man like Demetrio Toscani wielded immense power. The Carver couldn't have picked a better associate.

"I'll see you around," Garrity said.

Garrity and the other men kept their eyes on Silence as they retreated into the ruins of the Trav Hotel courtyard and vanished.

For a moment, Silence was frozen there, Beretta lowered at his side, ready for one of them to pop back out. Then there was movement in his periphery. He turned.

Judkins stood outside the Spirit, frantically waving his hands in broad strokes, yelling, trying to get Silence's attention. In one hand, he held a cellular phone.

CHAPTER TWENTY-FIVE

THE LATEST PHONE call was still echoing through Don's mind —the second call from Kendall.

Earlier, the first time she called, she'd been urgent but almost excited as she explained the piece of information she'd found—the note that included the name *TRAV HOTEL*.

But when she called him again, a few minutes earlier while Don waited for Max in Cerise Hillman's Dodge at the Trav, having using Kendall's intel, she had been in tears. He'd heard her car's engine blaring in the background. She wouldn't tell him much, only to meet her at Dew Hill Park.

Now he saw her just ahead of him, sitting on a bench. Legs crossed and hunched over, folded in on herself. It was the first time he'd seen her in weeks.

He, Max, and Cerise rushed across Dew Hill Park, a small but well-maintained green space of lush gardens, bright flowering plants, and neat pathways winding through the trees. They stopped in front of Kendall's bench, and she stood up, wobbling slightly.

Don reached out for her, grabbed her arm to stabilize her, but quickly turned it into a hug, pulling her in tight. She wrapped her arms around him, hugged back. But something was off. There was no energy in her.

Dark potentialities swarmed Don's consciousness. He pulled away from her, looked her straight in the eye, obscured by large sunglasses. Her cheeks were moist from recent tears, and the left side was flushed pink.

Don's hands were still on her shoulders, and he gave them a gentle squeeze.

"Are you hurt?" he said.

"I'm fine," Kendall said and nodded, her voice throaty.

Max stepped closer. "May we see it?"

Kendall nodded again and reached into her purse, took out a folded piece of paper that she handed to Max. Don finally took his hands off her shoulders and went over to Max, looked at the paper. There were shapes, drawn in pencil—a triangle and two different squiggle marks.

"It's what I saw in his notes," Kendall said. "I drew it from memory, but I think I got it about right."

Max turned to Cerise, who had already taken a book from her bag, flipping through the pages. He handed the paper to her.

"Does this make..." he said and swallowed. "Sense to you?"

Cerise nodded, placing the scrap of paper onto the page to which she'd turned. She squinted in concentration.

"I think so. Let me take a look."

As she turned away, Max took a step closer to Kendall.

"What's the man like?" he said and swallowed. "Ian Dalton."

Kendall's face darkened.

"A monster. Nothing but unrestrained hate. The kind of person who hates everyone but himself, someone with a chip on his shoulder carved out by the whole damn world."

Her nostrils flared.

"He was a spec screenwriter in L.A. Years ago. 'Speculation.' That's when a script is written not on commission, but with hopes of being purchased. Lots of them never get made into movies. He told me all about it. He did well for a few years, but fizzled out. Now he blames the people back in L.A. for his failures. And he ... he just *hates*. He hates, you know?"

She stopped and looked at Max, then Don.

"He hates *everyone*. His neighbors. The people in Reno. The people in L.A. And he..."

She trailed off, pausing again.

"He brainwashed me into thinking I can do no better than sleeping with him for money. I'm not going to lie; I found him intriguing at first. Oddly attractive. But ... then he started telling me that no one else would pay me as well as he does, that if I really cared about Cooper, I'd try to make the most money I could to take care of my sick dog, and ... And I believed him. *Oh, God, I believed him!*"

She looked up, locked eyes with Don. Her eyes were wet.

"Don..."

He put his hand on her shoulder.

...and noticed something strange—a sheen on the skin outside her eye, glistening in the sunlight. He just looked at her for a moment, frozen. Birds chirped in the branches above. The sound of cars on the street. And finally, Don gathered his courage.

He slowly brought both of his hands toward Kendall's face and placed them on her sunglasses. She did nothing to stop him. He took the sunglasses off.

Don gasped.

She'd tried to cover it with the shades. She'd tried makeup, too, to no avail. A wide area of the skin surrounding her right eye was dark indigo. Puffy, swollen, with a glossy shine. The eyelids on that side were nearly shut, just a sliver of her eye visible, which was bloodied, deep red surrounding her brown iris.

With the oversized lenses removed, her entire face was revealed, and Don saw that her right cheek was bigger than the other. Pinker. With scratch lines.

Frantically, his eyes scanned over her, top to bottom. She wore long sleeves that, along with her jeans, hid most everything else—except the little pink marks on her neck, peeking out from the top of her collar. Don put a finger in the collar, gently tugged down.

An angry red hand mark covered the side of Kendall's neck.

Max rushed over. His enormous fingers were clenched in quivering fists.

"Who did this?" Max said. "Dalton?"

She nodded. Her eyes watered.

Max looked her over like Don had.

"Where else did..." he said and swallowed. "He hurt you?"

Kendall looked away.

"Everywhere..." she whispered.

Don gasped again. He reached out and took her shoulder, as much to stabilize himself as to console his friend.

Cerise approached. She'd now closed her book; it hung at her side. She stared, a sort of shocked pain in her eyes.

Max glanced at her, then back to Kendall.

"Have to get you..." he said and swallowed. "To a doctor."

"No!" Kendall said immediately and stepped toward him. "No, I ... I don't have insurance. And—"

Max raised a hand. "My organization..." he said and swallowed. "Will pay."

After a moment, Kendall nodded. "Thank you."

Max offered a smile. Don couldn't recall seeing him smile yet, and he would have thought it would look strange on that severe, brooding face of his. But it didn't. It was genuine, radiant.

"Come on," Max said and immediately turned, leading the group out of the park.

As they hurried down the path, Cerise rushed to Max's side. She'd already opened her book again, and she somehow managed to read and speed-walk at the same time.

She then snapped the book shut and looked up at Max.

"I can break this code."

CHAPTER TWENTY-SIX

DALTON SHOVED him against the trailer—*Bang!*—and the corrugated siding warbled. Brooks Garrity looked up with shock and a bit of fear, and Dalton immediately wiped the expression off his face, backhanding him hard.

Damn, that was nice. Delicious.

It was demeaning to slap a man, and Dalton had wanted to slap the shit out of Brooks Garrity's whiny, psychotic face for a loooong time, to degrade and humiliate the creep.

Brooks's hand went to his cheek. A drop of blood came from the corner of his mouth.

"*Another* stabbing, Brooks?" Dalton screamed and slapped him again. "*Calypso!* Are you freakin' kidding me? You killed the most well-connected lowlife in Reno besides Toscani himself!"

He gave Brooks another hard shove back into the wall.

Bang!

"But I've done more," Brooks pleaded. "We can salvage this. I told you, I got us a new connection. With Toscani!"

Dalton scoffed. "Yes, yes. So you said. Congratulations, moron, you used your idiotic Carver reputation to waltz into the home of the very person I'm trying to unseat. Don't you get it, you stupid piece of shit? The partners who gave me the heroin don't want to ally with Toscani. They didn't just know the supply was bad; *they freakin' poisoned it!* If Toscani's heroin addicts started dropping off, then his reputation would suffer, the people would come after him with pitchforks, the press and the police would swoop down on him."

Brooks's lip trembled. "But ... but I didn't know that! You never told me the drugs were poisoned. You just said that a lot of people would end up dying, overdosing."

"Of course I didn't tell you! The partners wanted someone in Reno they could trust. They heard my name through the lowlife grapevine, and I passed the physical distribution on to one of my knuckle-dragging landscape employees, the guy who told me he fantasizes about killing people. I thought you'd be perfect. Someone who could distribute the drugs and once the people started ODing—or, I should say, being poisoned—you'd get your sick thrills from that."

He paused to stare into Brooks.

"But, no, you had to start committing your stabbings, you goddamn freak. And a series of idiot mistakes later, Toscani knows my name, knows I'm the one in Reno who's been killing his clientele. You've ruined what we've spent months working on. All this is over because of *you,* Brooks Garrity."

He smacked his hand over Brooks's face, palming it like a basketball, and squeezed hard, into his bones.

"You're out now. You got that? You're out of my operation. Go back to Toscani and tell him you failed. You're done, Brooks."

Another slap. Harder.

Brooks's eyes still burned, still glistened. Anger formed on his face. Prideful, childish, chastised retaliation. He put up his fists.

"Uh oh!" Dalton said with a dark laugh. "You wanna duke it out, do you, Brooks?"

He laughed harder.

Then he reached his right hand into his pocket. With his other hand, he threw a punch at Brooks, going intentionally high. Brooks juked to the left to avoid Dalton's blow, as Dalton knew he would. Dalton moved to the right and pulled his hand from his pocket.

Brooks's eyes went wide. His body bent in half as he grabbed his wrist. Blood gushed through his fingers.

The knife was ungodly sharp. Split-a-hair sharp. Dalton had just finished sharpening it a half hour earlier.

It had sliced through Brooks's wrist with ease. The skin instantly splayed outward, revealing underlying tissues.

Brooks breathed deeply, rapidly as he looked up at Dalton. His face was already blanching.

"Look at that. A suicide attempt," Dalton snickered. He held up the blade, which now glistened deep crimson. "It's one of your knives. Kinda ironic. Guess you shouldn't leave your shit around my trailer. You've felt it today, haven't you? The noose tightening around your white trash neck."

Brooks shivered as he looked up at him. Blood continued to pour out of his wrist.

"You *know* Calypso was talking today after you visited her, before you offed her," Dalton said. "You *know* the scumbag side of Reno now has confirmation of the rumors, the description—white, five-foot-nine, sandy blond hair. And if they know, the cops know. So what are you gonna do, Brooks? Go to a hospital?"

He put a hand on the other man's shoulder and hunkered over to get closer. In a whispering tone, he continued.

"The only thing you can do is go to your new friend, Toscani. Get one of those famous mob doctors to stitch you up. And when you do, tell him that Ian Dalton isn't just some bum. I'm a true threat. I'm the man who carved the Carver."

He straightened and stared down at Brooks. As he took his hand off Brooks's shoulder, the other man lurched forward, bending, nearly toppling to the earth.

"Now get off my property."

Brooks didn't move, just stared up at him. There was hurt in his eyes, and he looked at Dalton with a mix of bewilderment and angered confusion. The idiot had idolized Dalton for over a year.

"What are you waiting for? Better hurry. You're turning white as a ghost."

Brooks quivered with a wave of pain, then turned and hobbled off, bent in half. A hunchback.

Dalton smiled.

He looked at the knife. The blade was covered in blood.

Dalton was wearing a Garcia Landscaping T-shirt. Filthy, torn in more than one location. It was little more than a rag.

He wouldn't wear dismal clothing like this when he got back to Los Angeles. His days of wearing rags were almost over.

So screw it.

He used the shirt like the rag that it was and cleaned the blade, wiping Brooks Garrity's blood away.

CHAPTER TWENTY-SEVEN

TOSCANI ALREADY KNEW the man was coming to his office. Arturo had buzzed the intercom from the front gate and relayed the situation.

But Toscani was still shocked by what he saw.

The office door flew open, and in stumbled Brooks Garrity. Behind him was Arturo. Garrity was in a sorry state. His shirt was soaked with sweat. He clenched his wrist. There was blood everywhere.

Toscani rose. "What the hell is this? Did you try to off yourself?"

"No! It was Ian Dalton!" Brooks moaned loudly and stumbled toward the desk. "*Help!* God, it hurts! I'm ... I'm fading. Please, help me!"

He screamed again, and the sound echoed off the walls, off all the glass adornments and the shelves of books in Toscani's office.

Toscani's expression hardened. He had not forgotten Brooks's boldness from earlier—the young man had been foolish enough to tell him he was working for a man named

Ian Dalton, the person he said had distributed the killer heroin.

And now Brooks had stumbled into Toscani's office, claiming Dalton tried to kill him.

Toscani strolled casually to the hunched, convulsing man dripping blood all over his beautiful hardwood floors. But instead of pity, a kind of knowing confidence came to Toscani.

"Only hours ago you offered me a partnership with Ian Dalton," Toscani said. "But if his principal lieutenant, the Carver, was out knifing people, potential customers, I'm thinking Dalton doesn't want a partnership. Correct? Instead, he wants to run me out of business."

"That's right, but—" Garrity stopped and screamed. A moment later, gasping, he continued. "But I swear, I didn't know! That's why he did this. I ..." He groaned. "I want to join you. I can help you bring him down." Another scream. "It hurts! Shit, it hurts!"

Toscani tsked. "*This* is the mighty Carver? Sad."

Garrity looked up at him. His face was entirely blanched, his eyes wet.

"I can help you," Toscani said. "And—"

"*Please!* Yes, help!"

Toscani offered a patient grin.

"I can help you," he repeated. "If you prove your loyalty. And I don't think I need to remind you of what I'm capable of should you try to double-cross me."

Garrity nodded, stumbled, nearly fell over, grabbing a chair before he did. Noises came from his mouth, like incomplete dry heaves. His head tottered.

"I ... I swear to you," he puttered.

Toscani grinned. "Good. You'll start tonight. Your wound doesn't warrant all this bellyaching. We'll stitch you up, pump some pain meds in you, and then you're going to eliminate this threat you helped bring into my life. The two men who came into my office earlier—one was Ian Judkins. I'm sure you've heard of him. A lousy deadbeat. Somehow the guy got himself involved with a shadow man, some sort of alphabet agency guy, I'm thinking. His name is Max."

He narrowed his eyes at the squirming man before him, his face blanching rapidly, approaching death, the sort of man in a bind where he'll do *anything* to survive.

"You're going to find Judkins and Max. And then you're going to use your prodigious skills, Mr. Carver, to kill them both."

CHAPTER TWENTY-EIGHT

THE SEAT CUSHION was all but nonexistent, and the chair's metal frame was poking Silence's ass. The medical clinic was a less than stellar place, which meant that the waiting room's amenities weren't exactly comfortable.

But to maintain their under-the-radar nature, the Watchers often utilized humble resources, despite having nearly unlimited funds. In this case, to maintain anonymity, Silence had taken them to a downtrodden part of town where there was an equally downtrodden clinic, one that accepted cash and asked few questions.

It was all worth it. Because Kendall Anson was getting the help she needed.

At the other side of the waiting area was the doorway leading to the exam rooms. The door was open, as was the door to the exam room at the end of the hall, and Silence could see Kendall and Judkins in the room. Kendall was seated on the tall exam table; Judkins was on the chair below. Kendall had requested that he come with her for the exam, and the staff had accommodated. The doctor was no longer in the room, and now the pair was deep in conversation. From the looks of it, it was an earnest one.

Cerise was seated next to Silence, and they had the waiting room to themselves, aside from the outline of a woman in scrubs behind a sliding opaque glass window at the check-in counter. Faded yellow walls bore tattered posters featuring medical advice from years gone by, and the floor tiles were stained and chipped. The air was stuffy, stale, and smelled of bleach and antiseptic.

Cerise had her book open on one thigh and a notebook on the other. She'd been scribbling furiously since they sat, her brow furrowed.

Silence watched. He remembered how smart and capable she had been in Spokane. Yes, that much he could remember. But he'd forgotten her tenacity. Or had he noticed it at all the first time? Had this tenacity existed two and a half years ago, or had time changed her? He suspected she'd always been this way. It seemed to fit her.

She stopped then and placed her pencil down. She used both hands to rub her temples, grimacing. Stretched. Sighed.

She turned to Silence and looked at him for a long moment. Blinked. "This reminds me of Spokane. Gah, what a brain-buster. Gotta be honest, though. As dangerous as Culverson was, I actually had a good time breaking his code." She gave a small laugh. "Remember when we were up all night at the diner with the dictionary and the case files?"

Silence shook his head. "No."

Cerise's smile lessened, and she twitched. A bit of hurt in the eyes as well.

"That's right. You don't," she said and turned, looking through the open doorway and into the hallway beyond. "By the way, I did it. I took your advice. I contacted Hagan. Made things right." She paused, turned back to him. "But you don't remember that, either."

Silence shook his head. "Sorry."

"Not at all?"

Silence shook his head.

"You helped me out, talked me through a ... situation I was having, something not involved with the mission. We talked for over an hour." She smiled with reminiscence. "Even with your poor throat. You kept drinking water. I can't believe ... I mean, I wish you could remember."

She ran a finger along her notebook, watched it.

"You ... held me."

Silence shifted. He wanted to call out to C.C., but he restrained himself. One of the techniques C.C. had taught him was that of accepting one's inner sensations, to recognize them and let them be, to observe them.

He observed his inner self then. It was uncomfortable. He didn't want to picture himself in an embrace with this woman, helping her through what seemed to have been some sort of personal, non-mission-related ordeal.

As Cerise watched her finger, she brought it to her pencil. She picked the pencil up and went back to work.

Silence exhaled.

There was a water cooler on the other side of the room with a dispenser of cone-shaped paper cups. He was parched. But he didn't need water. He needed a Heineken.

Cerise's work had returned to a frenzied pace, and her pencil scratched like mad. Suddenly, she stopped and turned to him with a triumphant smile.

"I broke the cipher," she said. "It was a humdinger, dagnabbit, but I broke it!"

Humdinger. Dagnabbit.

She used old-fashioned words like that. Silence remembered that now, too, this quirk of hers. It came back to him, fully formed, gusting into his memory.

She used the old-fashioned words with an air of

purposeful eclecticism, but she did it so often that it became natural, a part of her, less ironic and almost genuine, endearing.

"So what do..." Silence said and swallowed. "The codes mean?"

"They translated into several more words. Unless these words make any sense to you on a surface level, I think we have another layer of the puzzle." She consulted her notes. "*Moon. Cup. Beast. Fund.*"

Silence brought a hand to his jaw and tilted his gaze to the stained ceiling above. He tried the words on.

Moon.

Cup.

He attempted visualization, working through the code in a way that C.C. would have approved of. He went to the abstract, picturing a cartoonish image of the moon sitting in a drinking cup, its circumference filling the cup's rim, like a scoop of ice cream in a bowl.

Or something different.

Beast?

Maybe a beast drinking from a cup. In a nighttime scene, bathed in *moon*light.

But, *fund?*

It was the most abstract of the words. Since the other three words were nouns, he suspected *fund* to be used as a noun as well, not its verb form. Still, *fund* was a less tangible noun than *moon*, *cup*, or *beast*.

What could he picture as a representative of the word *fund?* A bank account?

Yes.

He focused.

The dog—or maybe a cat; hell, a bear; it didn't matter, just a placeholder animal—drinking from a cup, with the moon, outside a bank.

Or maybe that was the wrong kind of *fund*. Maybe it was meant to be more abstract. Maybe the code-maker had been referring to *fund* as a general supply, like a *fund of knowledge*. This could mean that—

C.C. spoke to him. *Love?*

Yes? his mind's voice replied.

Calm your thoughts. You're looking at this from the wrong perspective. Keep going like this, and your mind is going to tumble into a tempest. Deep breath.

Silence closed his eyes. Took a deep breath. Sensed it in his sinuses, neck, lungs, returning to his neck, out his mouth, past his lips, gone.

A two-second meditation.

C.C. smiled and left.

She'd said he was looking at the code wrong. He scrapped his visualizations, pulled his eyes away from the drop-tile ceiling, looked at the notebook on Cerise's lap, found her list of words.

Moon

Cup

Beast

Fund

The worst-case scenario was exactly what Cerise had implied a few moments earlier—that this would be simply another layer of code, that there would be another set of messages to decipher past these.

But Silence didn't want to believe that. He *couldn't* believe it. Reno had reached a boiling point. Things couldn't go on like this.

Perhaps the words were replacements or parallels, not literal representations, not another layer of cypher codes. He let his eyes roam the list, falling on the "easiest" of the four —*beast*.

Animal, of course, was the natural replacement.

But the others?

Moon? What the hell could replace that? It seemed like a pretty damn definitive word, so maybe the other word would be more abstract. Like, *orb* or *sphere.*

He thought again of the notion of parallels rather than true replacements.

Star, perhaps?

Cup. Replacements. *Mug. Glass. Goblet. Chalice.*

Chalice!

"I have it!" Silence said.

Cerise spun in her seat, squaring up to him.

"Moon. Cup. Beast. Fund," he said and swallowed. "Starlight. Chalice. Animal. Charity." Another swallow. "Nevada Friends of Animals charity event." Another swallow. "At the Starlight Chalice Casino & Resort."

Cerise gasped. "Something's going to happen at the event?"

Silence nodded.

"When is it?"

Silence looked at the clock on the far wall, then back to Cerise. "In an hour. Come on!"

He hopped out of his seat, and Cerise followed him as he rushed across the waiting room and through the open doorway into the clinic. He heard the glass window slide open behind them, and the woman at the counter yelled out, "Hey! You can't go back there!"

They rushed into the exam room. Kendall and Judkins both looked up, surprised.

"It's tonight. Whatever they've..." Silence said and swallowed. "Been building up to will be—"

He stopped. Cerise had grabbed his arm.

"Stop. Save your voice," she said. She turned to the other two. "Something is going to happen at the charity event at the Starlight Chalice. He and I need to get there right now."

Silence spun on her.

Cerise looked up at him.

"Hey, there could be more codes," she said and shrugged. "You might still need your cryptographer consultant."

Silence wanted to object. But he knew Cerise was headstrong, just like him. He remembered that part, too.

So he gave a reluctant nod.

He looked at Judkins. "Take care of your friend."

"Of course."

Silence addressed Kendall next.

"Be safe. He might..." he said and swallowed. "Come after you."

"Ian?"

Silence nodded.

Kendall gave a defeated nod. "I ... I can't believe I got myself involved with someone like him. I hope none of you think too poorly of me. I knew he was a bad person, but I never thought he was truly evil."

Suddenly, her sad looked vanished, and panic took its place. She jumped off the exam table.

"Careful!" Judkins said.

She looked at Silence with wide, terrified eyes. "He's capable of anything, isn't he? Remorseless."

Silence nodded.

"Do you think ... I mean, if he's willing to hurt me, do you think he'd do something to my dog?"

Silence didn't respond.

"Oh, my God! He's there alone. Cooper! I left him alone. How could I be so careless?"

She snatched her purse off the counter and pushed past the others.

"Kendall!" Judkins called.

But she was already down the hallway. She rushed through the doorway into the waiting room and was gone.

CHAPTER TWENTY-NINE

DALTON'S PHONE RANG. He knew who it was before he answered.

"Hello?"

"What the hell is going on?" Wallace Boyd spat. "Please tell me that the Reno loser rumor mill is incorrect, that the Carver *didn't* knife Calypso."

Dalton took a deep breath, trying to steady himself. He hated being chastised, being treated like a child, but he couldn't express anything of the sort at the moment—he was entirely at Boyd's mercy.

And he had to keep his focus on his ultimate goal.

Back to your old life.

This is just a speed bump.

A nearly-decade-long speed bump.

Los Angeles.

L.A.

"He did," Dalton said, and quickly, before Boyd could reply, he added, "I know, Boyd. It's an absolute catastrophe. But I—"

"You're damn right this is a catastrophe!" Boyd said. "The

other partners are ready to pull out, but I convinced them to hold on for just one more day, to see what you can accomplish with the symbols. Has Garrity determined their origin?"

"Brooks Garrity is no longer part of this operation."

"You cut the Carver loose?" Boyd screamed. "Rumor says he also made a connection with Toscani."

"He did."

"You've got to be kidding me..."

Boyd sounded on the verge of detonation.

Dalton didn't immediately reply. By now, he knew Boyd well enough to understand there were times the guy simply had to vent. Grouchy old shits were like that. Dalton needed to let this moment breathe.

A long exhale hissed through the receiver, then Boyd said, "I'm putting a lot of faith in you, Ian Dalton."

The words hadn't sounded enthusiastic. Rather, there had been a deadly tone to them. The implication was clear.

The statement had actually been a threat.

What that threat was, Dalton couldn't be sure. But he could wager a guess...

Boyd would have him killed if this didn't work out.

Dalton swallowed hard, then said, "And that trust won't be abused, Boyd. I swear it. Listen, I know why things are falling apart, and it's not just Garrity's fault. There's this slut I know; she's been snooping around, got into my desk. I think she may have contacted someone. But I'll take care of her. I can make this right. I have an idea, a way to—"

"Screw your idea," Boyd growled. "We're meeting again. You, me, and the partners. Tonight. In public—at the charity event at the Starlight Chalice."

"But—"

Click.

Boyd was gone.

"Shit!"

Dalton slammed the receiver down.

For a moment, he just stared through the curtain to Hal's trailer beyond, and he felt the weight of Boyd's implication. A pulse of fear rushed over him.

But as quickly as it had come, he shook the fear off, literally giving his head a couple of shakes.

He grinned.

Boyd... the fool. Boyd was the principal coordinator of the operation, but he was rich. And sheltered. Out-of-touch. He hadn't gotten his hands dirty like Dalton had.

Dalton would soothe the old man's fears tonight at this meeting. The man had sounded pissed, murderous, but Dalton could tame him.

Nonetheless, it never hurt to be prepared, to have a backup plan.

He was going to take someone with him to the meeting tonight.

But first, he had to capture the person.

A grin formed as a plan fell together in his mind.

CHAPTER THIRTY

THE LIGHTS WERE OFF in Toscani's office. A small television was on a wheeled cart in front of his desk, and it put out a flickering glow that cast long shadows from all his chic adornments. He held an ink pen—24K gold, purchased in Italy a year and a half ago—and rolled it over his fingers slowly. Some distant, subconscious part of him enjoyed the exquisite surface of the metal, even during this dire moment. Arturo stood behind him.

The newscaster was finishing her report. She spoke of how the police were still baffled by the Carver and how they were beginning to believe the notion that had earlier been refuted—that the slayings and the rash of drug deaths were related. Though there had been no definitive connections to Reno's notorious criminal kingpin Demetrio Toscani, police were monitoring the man carefully.

She'd said his name no less than five times during the report. Toscani was accustomed to people using his name in the city of Reno. Typically with fear. Always with reverence. But these days, when his named was uttered in connection to a serial killer and to cheap, lethal drugs, it sounded bad. He hated hearing it come out of that bitch's lips.

...*Toscani*... she said again.

Toscani snatched the remote off his desk and smashed the red button on top, jabbing it toward the television like a fencer. With a pulse of light, the newscaster was gone. The screen went black.

"Hey, maybe if you turn the Carver in, they'll give you a key to the city," Arturo joked from behind.

Toscani slowly turned on his lieutenant, scowled at him, and threw the remote back onto his desktop.

"It wasn't a business deal that made me join forces with that lunatic. It was a survival move. If he's telling the truth, then he'll put an end to the flow of rotten heroin before this entire thing gets out of hand."

He pointed at the television for emphasis, then paused to roll the luxurious pen over his fingers, watching the glisten of soft light on its highly polished surface.

"It was a gamble, trusting the most notorious criminal this city has ever seen. But Reno's a gambling town, isn't it?"

Arturo chuckled.

Toscani gave the pen a final twirl, then placed it on the desk and looked up at his guard.

"Now we'll just have to wait and see how good of a gambler I am."

CHAPTER THIRTY-ONE

THE AUDI'S engine roared as it flew west on Interstate 80. The landscape blurred past on either side. While they were in the clinic, the sun had begun its departure, and the sky was turning pinkish-orange, edging the mountains in the distance with a brilliant radiance.

Silence glanced over at Cerise in the passenger seat, her face illuminated by the glow. She was staring out the window. She sighed.

"That poor woman," she said.

Undoubtedly, she meant Kendall Anson.

"Judkins is going…" Silence said and swallowed. "To help her."

Before they left, Judkins had been in a panic. He'd wanted to go after Kendall, but he couldn't go with Silence and Cerise —the Starlight Chalice Resort & Casino was in the opposite direction as Kendall's home, and the charity event was in less than an hour. There wasn't time to drop him off.

So as Silence and Cerise left, Judkins had been on the phone, making arrangements to borrow someone's vehicle.

Somebody he knew. A friend-of-a-friend-of-a-friend sort of situation.

Judkins was a weasel, no doubt about it. But he was a good man underneath. Silence was good at reading people. Judkins loved his friend, Kendall; he would look out for her.

Cerise turned to Silence then.

"I can't believe we're doing this again," she said, smiling, her voice shimmering with a bit of excitement.

"Doing what?"

"This." She gestured to the speeding car. "My heart's pounding. I'm guessing you don't remember taking me on a breakneck drive across Spokane on I-90 in a Miura?"

Silence's eyes lit up.

"I wish!" he said and swallowed. "I drove a Lamborghini Miura?"

Cerise nodded.

Silence said, "Damn! How did—"

"It's a long story."

Ugh. That was a memory Silence *really* wanted—driving the world's first supercar, a stone-cold classic manufactured from 1966 to 1973. Maybe it would be one of the memories that would come back to him, like Doc Hazel had mentioned. Hopefully.

"I want you to know," Cerise said, "that I really appreciate your getting me through the tough spot back then. Especially, when you..." She trailed off, paused. "Held me."

A memory flashed back to Silence. But it wasn't of a Lamborghini Miura.

Silence was shirtless.

Cerise's hand was on his shoulder.

Silence gasped.

Cerise kept saying that he had "held" her.

Could that mean...?

Shirtless.

Hand on his bare shoulder.

Silence shook his head.

No.

A hug. It had been a hug. She'd said so herself back at the clinic. It was unrelated to the bare-shoulder touch.

"I was just completing..." Silence said and swallowed. "My mission. A hug can be..." Another swallow. "Prudent and nothing more."

Cerise shuddered.

Silence turned, looked.

Her eyes had filled with tears.

"You're a jerk," she said and turned to the window again. She continued to speak without facing him. "Maybe you didn't just hug me. Huh? Think about it."

No.

No, Silence *wouldn't* think about it.

Shirtless.

His fingers clenched tight on the leather-wrapped steering wheel.

And his mind raced.

While he normally had a difficult time controlling his brain, even with the methods C.C. had taught him in his former life before the Watchers, this mission had been particularly taxing on his overactive mind space. Resurfacing amnesia memories will do that to ya.

But what memories were yet to resurface?

If and when they arrived, were they to be trusted?

Because Silence knew—*knew*—that Cerise's implications were wrong. Silence had slept with many prostitutes since he joined the Watchers, but they'd been forced on him.

He would never sleep with anyone else. Especially not a client.

He was true to C.C. beyond her death.

As the Audi barreled forward, Silence continued to wrestle with his mind.

CHAPTER THIRTY-TWO

KENDALL'S HANDS shook on the steering wheel as she sped her Geo Metro up the hill, throwing a dust cloud behind her on the gravel road that led to her community.

All kinds of thoughts had raced through her mind during the frantic drive from the clinic. She'd thought of Shaila, her friend in Las Vegas. Shaila had told her that she and Cooper always had somewhere to stay in Vegas. Kendall could start a new life like so many had down there in Sin City.

But most of all she'd thought about Cooper. Reno, Vegas, or Timbuktu—it didn't matter where Kendall went; she wasn't going anywhere without Coop.

The dog had been a source of comfort during her toughest times. She refused to let cancer take him away, and even more so, she would not allow anyone else to harm him.

Back at the clinic, when she'd asked Max if her dog might be in danger...

He'd not answered, but his non-response had said everything. It had been blunt. Blunt, but truthful.

This had made her predict the worst. It led her to an envisioned future where Dalton had hurt Coop, put hands on him, like he'd done earlier to Kendall.

Paranoia. Surely she was just being paranoid. Yes, it was the panic, the adrenaline blasting images her way. Images of pain in Coop's eyes, the same pain she'd seen in those eyes a year ago, the pain that had first made her take him to the veterinarian.

Or something even worse. The image of a motionless, furry body lying on her front lawn.

No.

She just had to stay focused, stay in the here and now, in reality and not a false vision of the worst possible.

She would grab Coop and a few essentials, and she would flee the city. She'd go to Shaila, to Las Vegas. She would get far away from everything that had closed in upon her here in Reno.

But as her car climbed the hill and the dilapidated house at the top came into view, Kendall's heart sank.

Ian was on her property, behind the chainlink fence, crouched over and petting her dog. His hand was atop Coop's head, fingers tussling the brown-and-white fur. The kennel door was open in the back of the yard. Evidently, none of the neighbors hadn't been alarmed. Why would they be? Ian had been over multiple times to screw her for fifty bucks.

His Chevy Citation was parked to the side of the property.

Her blood went cold at the site of Ian's hands on Coop.

Kendall slammed on the brakes and leapt from the car.

"What are you doing here?!" she shouted, her voice trembling.

Ian straightened and smiled, the expression looking almost predatory.

"Come with me, Kendall," he said calmly. "That's all you have to do."

A knife handle was visible at his belt, and he subtly indicated that he'd stab Coop if Kendall didn't comply.

Kendall shuddered. She stared at him, her chest heaving as she gasped for breath. She knew she had no choice.

She nodded.

Ian smiled again, then left Coop alone, exited the property, closing the gate behind him, and led her to his Chevy.

"Get in," he said.

CHAPTER THIRTY-THREE

"THERE IT IS," Silence said.

They had just turned a corner, and the tower appeared ahead, the tallest in the vicinity.

Sleek, modern. Mirrored glass and loud blue lighting tracing up its height. A large crowd was gathered under the porte cochère—which was brightly lit as the surrounding sky grew dimmer, oranger with the setting sun—and more people were filtering in off the sidewalks. Large, angular lettering proclaimed, *STARLIGHT CHALICE RESORT & CASINO.*

Silence felt the ripple of adrenaline surge through his arms, his legs. This had been a confounding mission—one in which he'd not even seen his nemesis, Ian Dalton, not even seen a photograph of him—but he sensed the anxious tingle of excitement that came when justice was finally drawing near.

Still, there were nagging thoughts tugging at him, stupid emotions to cloud his reason. He'd been trying to resist thinking about what Cerise had said on I-80, focusing on the mission, as he should, but the thoughts had kept intruding. He needed to excise them.

The light ahead turned red, and Silence brought the Audi to a stop. He took advantage of the opportunity and turned to Cerise. She faced him as well.

"My organization forces me..." he said and swallowed. "To sleep with prostitutes."

"O...kay..." Cerise said and raised an eyebrow. "Eww. Gross."

"And I use my mind..." Silence said, swallowed. "To imagine my fiancée..." Another swallow. "And escape."

Cerise blinked. Her lips parted. "Um ... why are you telling me this?"

"What I'm saying is..." Silence said. "If we slept together like..." He swallowed. "...you implied, I must've thought..." Another swallow. "You were a hooker."

Her lips parted again. A small sound came out. Then she scowled.

And slapped him.

Hard.

His face swung to the side. His cheek burned fire.

"Asshole! *I'm not a hooker.*" She crossed her arms over her chest. "Drive."

Silence looked at her, confused by her last word, cheek burning.

Then he saw the green light ahead. Someone behind him honked. He took off.

"Look, I never said we slept together," Cerise said. "Like you said, I *implied* it because you were being a jerk. But that was wrong of me. And I apologize." She sighed. "We didn't sleep together. We kissed."

A quick wave whooshed through Silence, high then low—first, relief that he hadn't slept with Cerise; then a gut punch.

She'd said they kissed.

She'd sounded entirely sincere.

Silence's mind teetered again, like it had on the Interstate,

ready to topple over. This time, though, the mission was literally right in front of him—with the Starlight Chalice tower
filling the windshield as the Audi progressed—and he refocused on the critical matter.

CHAPTER THIRTY-FOUR

BROOKS WAS DISGUSTED WITH HIMSELF, having this lousy Italian galoot driving him around.

He was in the passenger seat, and behind the leather-wrapped steering wheel was a massive man wearing a tight-fitting blue suit. He had a Rottweiler face that bore a prominent scar over his right eyebrow. His name was Arturo, Brooks had recently learned.

If this was the caliber of man that Brooks would be working side-by-side with in his upcoming employment with Toscani, then he shuddered at the implications. Sure, the money was undoubtedly going to be great, but if he was selling his soul to work among the degenerate masses he despised so much—to the point where he'd killed several of them for sport—then he might as well write himself off as a sellout.

Refocusing, he took his attention back to the road, peering through the Alfa Romeo's windshield.

"It should be up this hill," he said, pointing.

Arturo turned off the main road onto a gravel single-lane

that led up a stony embankment dotted with low-end houses. Brooks saw, halfway up, the house they were looking for.

"So who is this chick?" Arturo said.

"Kendall Anson. Judkins's friend. He's got a pathetic, middle-aged crush on her. If anyone knows where to find him, it's her."

Brooks had been to Kendall Anson's rental house once before, over a year ago, shortly after she'd started working at Garcia Landscaping, back when she was almost full-time, before Dalton had begun cutting her hours so that he could trap her into their current prostitution situation.

It had been a small gathering. A picnic. For a half dozen of her new coworkers at Garcia—including Brooks, Dalton, and Donnie Judkins. She'd been so proud to show off her dog. A *sick* dog, no less. The thing had cancer.

Someone with a soft heart would have found the scene touching. Brooks, though, had found it pathetic. Kendall Anson's pathetic, weak qualities were exactly what Dalton had exploited. Brooks didn't pity the idiot whore.

The house came into view around a slight bend in the sparse gravel road. It was just like Brooks remembered it—a one-story, ranch-style, falling-apart piece of nothing on a slab of rock surrounded by a sad chain-link fence. The cancer dog was behind the fence—loose, its kennel door open.

Kendall's Geo wasn't there; instead, there was a rusty Cavalier with a small dust cloud drifting away behind it in the gravel; it had just parked. The driver's side door opened, and out came Donnie Judkins.

"Well, look at that," Brooks said to Arturo.

Arturo gave the Alfa Romeo a bit more gas.

Judkins rushed toward the chain-link gate, yelling.

"Kendall! *Kendall!*"

Arturo brought the car to a slow stop, and Brooks lowered his window.

Judkins heard them, whipped around.

Brooks smiled, and he sensed his disingenuous but oh-so-useful amiability making an appearance on his visage.

"Hey there, buddy!" he said. "Haven't seen you in a while."

Judkins didn't respond. His body went rigid. The dog barked.

And Brooks kept smiling.

"Let's catch up; how about it?" He felt the fake smile drop from his face, and in a different tone, he growled, "Get in the car, Judkins."

CHAPTER THIRTY-FIVE

DALTON GRINNED as he tugged Kendall along by the hand.

The bitch had had the audacity to go through his desk. Like Brooks Garrity, she was another local loser who was threatening Dalton's plan, his way of getting out of this shit town and back to a real city. Kendall had been so bold, so sly, thinking she was a little detective.

But now Dalton had her by the hand, literally leading her along as they pushed through the busy early-evening sidewalks, going for the crowd at the brightly lit entrance of the Starlight Chalice tower ahead.

Kendall looked defeated, ready to die, with an ignorant, obedient expression on her face. She also seemed truly frightened—not of him, but of what might happen to her dog.

A goddamn dog!

Idiot woman. Dalton had known that threatening Cooper would impact Kendall, but he didn't think it would be *that* impactful. She was an emotional fool. It was no wonder she'd failed at life.

He gave her hand another tug. She stumbled to keep up with him.

"Remember, Kendall, we're just another happy couple out on the town, headed to the charity event to watch a bunch of big, stupid balloons light up and piss our money away on broken cats and limp horses and cancer-riddled dogs like yours. Got it?"

Kendall nodded, her eyes downcast.

"And should the need arise," Dalton continued, "you're going to be my human shield." He snickered. "These are some tough old salts, and if I don't impress them, I think they might wanna kill me."

He snickered again—a truer laugh, a Devil-may-care, end-of-the-world laugh.

Dalton was ninety-nine percent sure he could pull this off with flying colors. It was his usual confidence showing its usual colors.

Still, there was that one percent that produced visions of Boyd and the other two partners snapping their fingers, summoning unseen goons from the casino throngs, dragging Dalton off to a back-alley death.

He glanced over at Kendall.

Her eyes remained downcast. Defeated.

Pathetic.

All the same, she'd shown a bit of bravery lately with her wannabe detective work. That was impressive, in a way. He'd perused her cellular phone when he took it out of her purse, checked the call list. She'd dialed someone while she was at the trailer, someone with a local area code.

"Who did you call, Kendall? After you rummaged through my desk. The cops? The feds?"

Kendall said nothing.

Dalton snickered again. "All right, tough girl."

As they crossed another street, he turned and saw, in the distance at Rancho San Rafael Park, all those brightly colored hot air balloons lined up, ready to put on their show. A "balloon glow," it was called. An idiotic waste of time for idiotic people.

The tower was just ahead. Dalton reached into his pocket, pulled out the portable microcassete recorder. He pressed *REC*. The tiny red bulb illuminated, and the tape turned.

He put the device back in his pocket. Like the human shield, this was another means of covering his ass at the deadly meeting he was about to hold.

They reached the bright lights of the Starlight Chalice and slowed, joining with the crowd assembled there. The energy was slow and easy, full of laughter, and it took a while before they made it through the doors and into the building.

When they did, Dalton pulled Kendall along with him, past the lobby and into the casino, a gaudy place of chandeliers and red carpet and poker tables and blaring slot machines. The crowd was thick, and there were signs everywhere with the name of the charity event. Many of the people roaming the casino floor wore lanyards, which also bore the event's name—*NEVADA FRIENDS OF ANIMALS ANNUAL CHARITY*—in the same font as the signs. The air was alive with chatter and laughter, the clink of chips, the chiming of bells.

Dalton craned his neck and looked out over the undulating mass of bodies.

He spotted them.

To the left. Boyd and the fat one and the one with liver spots. They were behind a roulette table.

"Come on," he said to Kendall and pulled her through the crowd.

The old men saw him approach. Boyd smiled, a look that was warm on his lips, deadly cold in his eyes.

A few feet away from the partners, Dalton came to a stop. The older men wore tuxedos, and around their necks they wore the lanyards. All had drinks. All wore superior, smug grins.

Boyd stood slightly ahead of the other two. He gave Dalton a nod.

"Mr. Boyd," Dalton said.

Boyd's eyes went to Kendall. "Is this your wife?"

Dalton gave his response a moment's thought. "No, Boyd, this is the bitch I was telling you about, the one who's been snooping around. I think she might be a big part of our problems. You want her?"

He tugged Kendall by the hand, and she stumbled a few inches toward Boyd.

Boyd glanced at her. And didn't react. He just brought his gaze back to Dalton.

"It's over for you, Ian Dalton," Boyd said.

A stupid, reactive part of Dalton sent another wave of fear through his body with Boyd's words, picturing a gun or those goons he'd imagined earlier coming from the crowd to grab him.

After the adrenaline quickly washed through his system, he said, "What do you mean, Boyd?"

"I mean, you're done with our operation," Boyd said. "You distributed the poisoned heroin for us, but your ineptitude has shown that you're no leader. Now that the supply is in the streets, your services are no longer needed."

"But ... but I haven't deciphered the symbols! If you'll just—"

"*Symbols?!*" Boyd said with a loud, derisive laughed. "You don't even know what you're looking for, do you? You don't know what type of symbols those are."

Dalton just stared back at him, blinked.

"They're 'non-logographic geometric shapes,'" Boyd said, enunciating the name slowly, pointedly, like he was carefully reciting an esoteric term of which he had little familiarity. "Does that name sound familiar to you?"

It was a bizarre-sounding term—*non-logographic geometric shapes*—but in a perplexing way, it *did* sound familiar. He had no clue why.

"I ... um..."

"Oh, you stupid fool," Boyd spat, the last vestige of his fake smile vanishing. "*You* came up with the name yourself. For your screenplay. *The Egyptian Chronicles*. Remember?"

Dalton hardly remembered—he'd been baked out of his mind when he wrote that script—but he did. Yes, it had been one of his early attempts, an action-adventure script with a target audience of young adult. It was the second spec script he'd sold. He'd gotten 6K a year for five years for that piece of shit.

And there had been a component related to Egyptian hieroglyphs. A character had modified them into his own code system, devoid of their original meaning.

The character had called it a system of *non-logographic geometric shapes*.

Boyd snickered. "You don't even remember writing your own shit. *Gah!* You're just as washed-up as everyone says, aren't you? We arranged for the symbols on the syringes, similar to the ones described in your screenplay. It was a little trail for you to chase, a mystery to solve, that would eventually lead you here to this event. But you and your partner, the Carver, were too stupid to figure it all out." He paused. "Know why we did it?"

Dalton just looked back at him.

"Because if anyone *else* figured it out—say, the cops, for instance—they'd link everything together. See, if the Reno authorities deciphered the symbols, they would then connect them to the loser, washed-up screenwriter who originated them, the same wash-up who has an established reputation for dealing drugs on the side. Makes sense, doesn't it?, that a man like that would move on to dealing heroin and try to be sneaky about it by using a code system he created. You didn't figure out the symbols; the cops didn't figure out the symbols. So we moved things along."

Dalton stammered. "What are you ... What are you saying?"

Boyd grinned wickedly. "Someone made an anonymous call to the Reno police, explained the symbols and their connection to your shitty, forgotten screenplay." He paused. "You're ruined, Ian Dalton."

CHAPTER THIRTY-SIX

"WHAT ARE WE LOOKING FOR?" Cerise said.

"Not sure yet," Silence said as he scanned the crowd.

They were in the Starlight Chalice's main casino, which was crammed with people—half dressed black-tie style, the other casually dressed.

This place was more opulent, more old-fashioned and quintessential than the casino at the Horizon Palace where Silence had been staying. Gleaming crystal chandeliers hung from the ceiling, reflecting their light onto tables and machines. Electronic games and slot machines lined the walls, each vying for players' attention. Everywhere were easels with elegant yet simple signs declaring, *NEVADA FRIENDS OF ANIMAL ANNUAL CHARITY.*

Cerise had cracked the code, and Silence had deciphered its meaning. They'd found the right location.

Now what?

Silence's thoughts went back to the notion he'd had a few minutes earlier in the car—the fact that he had no clue what Ian Dalton looked liked. He'd not even seen a photo. That morning, at the cafe, Judkins had given a description. He'd said Dalton was an average-looking middle-aged guy who—

Kendall!

Silence spotted Kendall Anson. On the other side of the casino floor. She was with a man, and they were by a roulette table in conversation with a trio of older guys in tuxedos.

Kendall's companion was tall. Fifty something. Dark hair with white on the sides. White stubble beard. He wore a ratty green T-shirt, which looked out of place even among the more casually dressed people in the casino.

The T-Shirt said, *GARCIA LANDSCAPING SERVICES.*

Ian Dalton...

He and Kendall held hands, but by the panicked look on Kendall's face, it was clear this was not consensual. She was his prisoner.

Silence whipped around and found that Cerise, too, had spotted Kendall.

"Gotta go," Silence said.

She nodded.

Silence tensed, ready to run. Stopped.

He and Cerise locked eyes.

A moment passed.

Then Silence broke the stare, spun around, and bolted through the casino.

CHAPTER THIRTY-SEVEN

EVEN AFTER ALL SHE'D been through that day, Kendall knew things were now much worse. In fact, she was at the most dangerous impasse of her life, being pulled around town as Ian's prisoner, his literal "human shield."

But, still, she smiled.

Because Ian had just been thwarted.

When the three old men had revealed themselves as having double-crossed Ian, the look on her captor's face had been thrilling—an expression of bewilderment and confused, soul-crushing despair.

The one called Boyd continued to give Ian a look of superiority. "We'd like to thank you, Dalton. We've been trying to get a position in Reno for some time."

"I ... but..." Ian stammered. Kendall thrilled even more to see him struggle. "But *you're* from Reno."

Boyd shook his head. "That's what we told you. I'm from Phoenix. My friend here is from Oregon, and my other friend is from El Paso."

He gestured toward the other two men in turn as he mentioned them.

"We're only here to see these wonderful balloon races of yours," he said with an obnoxious, dark smile. "We had to make you think we're locals. Now that you've got us a foot in the door, we'll run the city from afar. Toscani's already toast. The cops and, more importantly, the media think our heroin that killed all those folks is actually Toscani's. Won't be long before we can sweep in and fill the power vacuum. Couldn't have done it without your help. Thank you."

All three men nodded enthusiastically, though their smiles were disingenuous, snide.

"You can't do this!" Ian said. "We had a deal."

"I can't?" He waved his hand left and right, indicating again the other two. "Each one of us is more powerful than Toscani in our home cities. Do you want to toy with us, Ian Dalton? Or do you want to leave right now with our gratitude for services rendered?"

Ian stammered again, trying to find something to say. Nothing came out. He looked at Kendall, then back to Boyd. He exhaled. Shook his head sadly. Then he grabbed her hand and turned around.

They started across the casino floor, heading back toward the revolving doors. With Ian's plan thwarted, Kendall couldn't begin to imagine what he had planned for her now. But at the moment, she wouldn't concern herself with the future, not even the immediate future. She was living in the here and now, savoring it.

It was a bad thing, what she was doing. There was a term for it: *schadenfreude*. German, she believed. The concept of gaining pleasure from another's misfortune. She'd always heard there were spiritual ramifications for schadenfreude. Bad karma.

Hell with it.

She was enjoying this.

To this point, Ian had manipulated, humiliated, and

abused her. Today, he'd taken hands to her and taken her hostage. And he'd threatened a cancer-stricken dog. All of these things made her realize that her months-earlier assessment had been way off. Ian Dalton wasn't just creepy; he was pure evil.

This revelation also told her he'd likely lied to her, that he hadn't had a reason to cut her hours at Garcia. He'd done that to con her into sleeping with him for money.

She thought of how it had happened. She'd started at thirty-five hours per week. Then thirty. Soon, it was down to twenty. Eventually, she wasn't even close to half-time.

Though the thought of this fueled a rage-filled fire inside her, at the moment, the more pressing concern was survival. He had already told her she was his human shield when he thought he was on his way to fulfill his destiny. Now, having his plan destroyed by the old men behind them, there was no telling what he would do to her.

Among the frenzied commotion of the casino floor around them, a particular motion caught her eye. Ian had noticed it too, and they both turned to look.

It was a large man in dark clothing, moving quickly through the crowd, way at the other end of the floor.

It was Max.

Kendall's mouth fell open. And she smiled.

With all the hell that was going on, with the uncertainty about Coop, with the discovery that her months-long companion, Ian, was a murderous lunatic, there was still no stopping her smile.

Because there was Max.

The man who had swooped in after the wake of Ian's attack and insisted she get medical attention, made the arrangements, paid for it.

The man whose genuineness had showed through his

stoic facade, even before dread flashed over his face at the sight of her wounds.

There he was. Pushing through the crowd in her direction, eyes locked on her, giving it everything he had.

She had seen tonight the lowest a man could be in the form of Ian Dalton, a man she'd known for over a year. But now, almost as if God wanted to show her the difference, she saw the best a man could be in someone she'd met that very day.

Ian slowed, squinting to look at Max as he pushed closer to them. "What the hell?"

He turned to Kendall. Then his eyes lit up with that fury that he got when he was disrespected. He'd seen her smile. She couldn't help it.

"Who is that man, Kendall?"

She didn't answer. She wouldn't. She just continued to smile.

He squeezed her hand hard enough to make her gasp.

"Who is that asshole?" He squeezed again, harder. The bones inside her hand pressed together. "What are you smiling about, bitch?"

She stepped into him, got on her tiptoes, as close to his face as she could. She spoke clearly, slowly, and loudly. "He's a friend."

She sneered at him.

That expression came to his face again, that confused expression, the same one he'd had when he was stammering back there with Mr. Boyd. He looked her up and down.

Then he turned back toward the revolving doors and ran, tugging her along with him.

CHAPTER THIRTY-EIGHT

BROOKS HELD A GUN—A Smith & Wesson 459.

He was reminded of the joy he'd felt while wielding knives, living his dream as the serial killer known as the Carver.

It had been his fantasy fulfilled, and he'd still been living the dream until that very afternoon when he'd killed Calypso and the two scumbags at the Trav.

Now, only a matter of hours later, everything had changed. The Carver fantasy was truly just that—a fantasy. Brooks had been betrayed, sliced, nearly died, and joined forces with the city's ruling crime boss. All in one day.

He looked down at his bandaged wrist.

Yes, it had been a hell of a day. He'd learned a lot. It was time to stop living in fantasy world.

It was time to grow up.

No more knives.

This 9mm pistol instead.

He gripped the handle, traced his finger along the trigger guard.

The night air was dry and cool. Sweat and apprehensive

energy lingered in the bustling downtown Reno nightlife. Neon lights. Inane chatter. Pods of ignorant wretches lurching along the sidewalks, preparing for an evening of watching pretty balloons then getting sloshed and pissing their money away.

Brooks hated the sensation, walking among them, but it was what he needed to do for his new position with Toscani. He followed the herd down the sidewalk with Donnie Judkins held captive beside him.

Judkins was a mess. A little while ago, Brooks had tortured him. His face was red and raw from the beating Brooks had given him. The beating hadn't taken long, though, until Judkins gave up the information—the location of his companion, Max.

If what Judkins said was to be believed, Max was going to the Starlight Chalice. Brooks couldn't be sure what in the world Max would be doing there, but he did know the Starlight was hosting a charity that evening. An animal charity. Maybe the mystery man was an animal lover. Maybe he had a real soft heart for cancer dogs, just like Kendall Anson.

Brooks was taking Judkins with him until he located Max. After he killed Max, he would kill Judkins. With both men dead, his first task for Toscani would be complete.

It would be a hell of a way to end a hell of a day.

Brooks had the Smith at his side, concealed beneath his hooded sweatshirt, and he walked closely to Judkins so that he could press the gun at the other man, remind him of the danger he was in.

As they followed the crowd around a corner, the Starlight Chalice Resort & Casino appeared ahead, a particularly stunning tower among Reno's many flashy casinos. Blue lights traced the corners of the the mirrored-glass facade. Signs near the entrance announced the charity event.

"You're sure this is where we'll find Max?" he hissed at Judkins.

"Yes," Judkins said. His tone was as beaten as his body. As soon as he'd given up Max's location, Brooks had seen the look of self-loathing on the face.

Brooks wasn't surprised, though.

Donnie Judkins had a reputation. A well-earned one. The reputation of a self-serving worm.

No wonder he'd betrayed his friend so quickly.

Brooks then nearly stopped, right in the middle of the foot traffic.

Because up ahead, there was ruckus in the crowd outside the Starlight. The commotion had been caused by a man running out of the revolving doors and down the steps.

It was Ian Dalton. He was moving quickly and tugging Kendall Anson along with him.

Shock and fury came crashing down on Brooks. Was this some sort of setup? Why was *Dalton* there at the Starlight Chalice in addition to Max?

Brooks quickly formulated the answer.

Toscani!

This was a setup. Toscani and Dalton must have been working together the entire time. This mystery Max person was evidently at the Starlight too, so that meant he must also be in on it.

The realization made the anger within Brooks swell. His grip tightened on the gun beneath his sweatshirt and he felt a wave of paranoia wash over him.

His vision blurred, and in that moment, he felt nothing but hatred for all humanity. All of the people around him on this crowded sidewalk were nothing more than pieces to be moved around on a board game. He wanted to take out his gun and shoot them all until they laid still by his feet like rag dolls.

Brooks wanted to do it so badly.

He almost did it.

But he restrained himself.

If he did it right now, some good Samaritan would take him down.

No, Brooks had to be more methodical about it.

He looked across the street. A three-story building. A gift shop at street-level. Apartments on the two floors above.

With balconies.

One of the apartment's on the third floor had darkened windows. Nobody home.

The balcony. That would be his vantage point. His roost. His hunter's stand. After he emptied his Smith into the crowd from the balcony, he would run back through the apartment to the fire escape in the back. As a local, he knew the building. He knew there was an alley behind it. As the Carver, he'd gotten a good sense of the network of alleys and escape routes in the downtown area.

He looked at Judkins, and by the other man's stunned reaction, it was clear that Brooks must look unhinged. He was no longer able to bend his visage to his will; his mania was out on display.

But that didn't matter.

Brooks *was* unhinged. If his life was really going to capsize in one day, then he was going to take a lot of innocent people out with him.

He dashed past Judkins and pulled the Smith out of concealment. Immediately, people saw the gun and screamed.

Brooks ran across the street. Cars screeching. Horns. Onto the opposite sidewalk. He pushed his way through the crowd. They were all staring at him with fright. There were screams. They darted away. He liked that. As manic and purposeful as he felt, he enjoyed frightening these degenerates.

Into the store. Full of junk. Foreign-made knickknacks. Soda and beer. A few outdoor supplies. He shoved aside the person blocking his path. A woman. She fell over. He was looking for access to the upper floors, the apartments. There had to be—

There. A door in the back.

He approached it. More people cleared out of his way. The person working behind the counter—a gangly woman with dark hair, too many wrinkles—approached him. "You can't go back there!"

He grabbed her by the face, extended a knee, and flipped her entire body back behind the counter. People in the store screamed. He turned the doorknob. Wouldn't budge. He kicked the door, hard. Once. Twice. The wood around the handle cracked. A third kick, and the door flew open, smacked into the wall.

Stairs in front of him, dark and dusty. He ran up them. Pivoted on the second-floor landing. And threw open the door onto the third floor.

A hallway with apartment doors. A musty smell. Marijuana smoke.

He found the door to the apartment he'd spotted from the street. Apartment 302. Tried the handle. Locked.

He kicked the door like he had the one in the back of the shop. This time, it took only one kick.

Whack!

The door flew open.

A ho-hum living room before him. At the rear, a glass door.

It went to the balcony.

He crossed through the space, opened the glass door, stepped outside, and looked down.

There they were.

Down there on the street.

They were the reason he'd fought his way up to this balcony.

Those people. Those swarming wretches.

He looked at them down there. So many of them. The entire area was crawling with them. He wanted them gone. He wanted them all gone.

Brooks scanned through the roaming, belching mass below him.

The last stand of the Carver. He was going to take as many of these shits out with him as he could.

He wrapped his finger around the trigger. Aimed the Smith at the crowd.

And someone grabbed him.

He turned around to find that someone had followed him through the apartment and grabbed his arm just before he could fire.

It was Donnie Judkins.

Struggling against Judkins's surprising strength, Brooks began to pull the Smith in his direction.

This was to be the Carver's last stand, and he wasn't going to let some goddamn loser spoil it.

CHAPTER THIRTY-NINE

DALTON GROWLED as he pushed through the people surrounding the Starlight Chalice's brightly lit entranceway. The area was absolutely packed with the nighttime crowd, spilling onto the sidewalk beyond, half of them dressed to the nines, the others dressed for a party, and all of them full of even more excitement than a normal Reno Friday night, buzzing with anticipation for the balloon glow.

Dalton kept Kendall's hand pinched tightly in his, enough that she could feel his threat, staying close beside her—just another happy, half-drunk couple out on the town.

He shoved through the crowd, going down the steps, moving as quickly as he could without drawing attention.

Kendall shuddered again as his hand tightened on her fingers when they descended the last step.

"Shut your mouth," Dalton hissed.

He looked over his shoulder, back to the revolving doors. The big man, Dalton's pursuer, wasn't there. But Dalton could feel the man's approaching presence. In one way or another, Dalton had been the prey many times throughout his life; he was quite familiar with this putrid sensation he was suffering.

But he could get out of this. As soon as he'd taken off from the Starlight Chalice, he'd already picked a place to run —the half-completed hotel/casino tower right beside the Starlight.

At the sidewalk, he tugged Kendall to the right, going for the tower. It was an unfinished monolith of gray, shooting imposingly high into the nighttime sky and the neon lights surrounding it. The exterior was rough, like an abandoned stone sculpture. Crates and scaffolding were scattered around the base, and dangling wires gave the tower an eerie feel.

He approached the orange plastic safety fence and climbed over, pulling Kendall with him. Some do-gooder from the sidewalk yelled at him. He ignored it. Dodging construction machines and piles of earth and concrete, they stepped through an open doorway into the building.

Before he turned the corner, he stole another glance back toward the Starlight.

No big man following them.

The air inside the place was dry, stagnant, dead. And chilly. He grasped Kendall's hand tighter and spun her against the wall hard enough to send a *crack* that reverberated harshly throughout the endless bare concrete. She screamed.

"Who was that man back there?" Dalton yelled. "Tell me! You recognized him."

She didn't respond, didn't look at him, just kept crying pathetically.

He slapped her.

"*Who is he?!*" Dalton screamed. "Is he a cop? What did you do? Who did you bring with you, you half-breed *goddamn slut!*"

He was about to slap her again, but then she looked up. He'd gotten through to the bitch. Her lip trembled as she brought her eyes back up to his.

She started to speak...

...and then rage flashed across her face as she crashed her knee into his crotch.

Dalton yelled out and nearly vomited. The pain shot through his entire body, buckling him at the knees. As he dropped, he clasped Kendall's wrist.

And after a second to recompose, he stood back up and shot a hand forward, grabbing her by the throat and slamming her back into the wall. She gagged and clawed at his hand as he squeezed harder, relentlessly.

He could have killed her then, wanted to kill her, to snuff her out.

But he stopped.

He released her throat.

She bent over much as he just had, coughing, a line of drool falling from her lips and puddling in the dust.

No, Dalton couldn't kill her. He still needed a human shield.

Tugging her wrist, he yanked her out of her bent-over position, and they went for the stairwell in the corner. It was empty, unfinished, no handrail. Their footsteps echoed.

Onto the second floor. He rushed them over to one of the open window frames. He looked down at the Starlight's entrance and the surrounding city—the multi-colored lights, the crowds on the sidewalks, the traffic.

No sign of the big guy.

He exhaled.

They could stay here for an hour. Maybe two. That would be enough time to—

Wait.

There!

The big guy.

Pushing through the throng outside the Starlight, stopping, scanning his surroundings frantically as if lost.

Dalton pulled himself to the side of the window frame, out of sight, yanking Kendall with him, and he peered around the edge of the concrete, looking at the man below.

"Up here!" Kendall screamed.

Dalton whipped around on her. She had her free hand cupped over her mouth.

He looked back outside.

The big guy was now sprinting toward the construction site. He hopped the plastic fence and looked up.

...and made eye contact with Dalton.

Dalton grabbed Kendall by the shoulders, digging his fingers in hard, gritting his teeth, and he stopped himself right before he tossed her out the open window.

He met her gaze—those brown eyes wide and filled with a strange mix of both defiance and dread—pulled back his arm, and backhanded her hard.

Her head flew to the side, hair whipping around, and she collapsed into a pile on the concrete.

Shit.

He'd let his emotions get the best of him. He still needed his human shield, and he'd just rendered it unconscious. Kendall lay completely motionless aside from the gentle rising and lowering of her chest.

Footsteps.

Dalton jumped over the body, going toward the stairwell, and planted himself against the wall.

More footsteps. Below. Slowing from a run. Approaching the structure. Coming off the torn earth outside and into the solid, hollow environment of the building.

Crunching. Getting closer.

Then speeding up again, coming at a run.

The footsteps entered the stairwell. Big, heavy, fast footsteps, growing louder.

Boom. Boom. Boom.

And then there he was.

The man ran out of the stairwell and stopped. They were a few yards apart. He held a pistol.

About six-foot-three. Tall, but not the tallest guy Dalton had ever seen. It was the proportions that made him look even taller than he already was. Broad shoulders above a tight waist, creating a dramatic V-taper. Long arms. Muscular legs. His face was all angles and choppy dark hair, a severe-looking customer, like an overgrown fashion model.

The man glanced at Kendall's unconscious body. When he looked back at Dalton, his teeth were bared, gritting, and his eyes burned. He raised his pistol and approached. Palpable fury coursed through his arms, which seemed taut with shaking restraint as he kept the gun leveled at Dalton.

Dalton raised his hands.

"You a cop? A fed?"

The man didn't respond. He kept coming at Dalton.

So Dalton began inching back.

"Who are you?" Dalton said.

Initially, it seemed like the man was again going to deny an answer, as though his anger was clouding his basic motor skills, but finally he said, "Max."

Shit! The guy's voice. Grumbling, crackling. So ruinous that if Dalton didn't know better, he would have assumed it had been created with some sort of modulator.

Dalton waited a moment as he continued to creep backward. "Just Max?"

Max didn't respond.

"Okay, then, Max. I'm Ian Dalton." He pointed to the unconscious whore behind them. "And it seems you've already met this lil angel."

He laughed.

Max did not.

Max was still approaching, getting closer. Still aiming his gun. Dalton could see his visage clearly now. Max's angular facial features Dalton had noticed moments earlier played art-show-style tricks in the multi-colored patches of light coming in through the open window frames.

As Max continued toward him, Dalton got the distinct impression that his main theory—that Max was a fed—was incorrect. No, this man meant to kill him, not arrest him. He must have been one of Toscani's; that's all Dalton could figure.

Whoever he was, the sight of the beaten whore had amplified his kill objective. The closer Max drew to him, the more Dalton could see the rage in his eyes, the hate, the desire to kill.

Survival. At this point, that was all Dalton had left. He would have to find a way to survive this.

First, he would try diplomacy.

"Shooting an unarmed man, then?" Dalton said, flicking his eyes side to side to indicate his raised hands.

Max shrugged, didn't stop his forward progress.

"I've done so..." he said and swallowed. "Many times before."

Shit...

Dalton gulped.

He felt the nearing presence of the back wall, and he stole a glance backward over his shoulder.

The wall wasn't as close as he'd thought, but he noticed something else.

Something much more important.

A large, rectangular cutout in the concrete floor, a few feet behind him. More than wide enough to accommodate his body. He assumed it was some sort of home to a future

HVAC system or other utility component or a stairwell between a two-story suite.

Whatever it was, it opened up to a small landing three feet down.

And on that landing was a foot-and-a-half scrap of rebar.

Dalton fought against a wicked, triumphant grin as he turned back around to Max.

He continued moving backward.

Max continued toward him.

Only a few more feet. But he had to be careful. The timing had to be perfect.

And he needed to hide his intentions, so he would keep Max talking.

"Then why not do it?" he said. "If you've killed many other unarmed men, why haven't you shot me already?"

He felt the presence of the cutout behind him.

Careful.

Careful...

"Need to know..." Max said and swallowed. "What *you* know." Another swallow. "Talk."

The cutout was right there, right behind him. The crunch of his footsteps took on a slightly different quality, echoing off the space below.

"What's to say?" Dalton said and shrugged his raised shoulders. "I know how to survive."

With that, he leapt back.

He caught a glimpse of Max's widening eyes just before he dropped. His stomach fell, and for a second, paranoia told him that his blind jump was going to lead him plunging down to unseen depths, lying in a cracked and ruined clump in the casino's future basement garage.

But three feet later, he allowed his knees to bend and absorb the fall. He grunted with the impact, and from his crouched position, he quickly located the length of rebar, snatched it up.

The Beretta appeared over the concrete edge above, followed immediately by Max's scowling face.

Dalton bolted up, swung the rebar.

And cracked Max across the jaw.

CHAPTER FORTY

DON WAS FIGHTING AGAIN.

His middle school self would be so proud.

He wasn't sure why he'd done it, *how* he'd done it, but somehow as soon as he'd seen Garrity yank his pistol out during his mad dash across the street, he'd chased after the man. Instinct had told him Garrity was about to unleash Hell.

First, he'd crossed through the store. Saw the frightened customers. The employee on the floor. The open door in the back.

He'd bolted through the door, up two flights of stairs, to a hallway, through another open door, through a darkened apartment, and through a final, open, glass door onto a balcony, grabbing Garrity from behind just as the lunatic was aiming his gun at the crowds below.

Someone saw the struggle and evidently saw the weapon, too, as there was a scream of, *Gun!*

Then more.

Shit, that guy's got a gun!

He's gonna fire!

But Garrity hadn't fired. Don had wrapped his arms

around the guy from behind, grabbing him at the elbows, and twisting him around so that the barrel was aimed back toward the building.

They'd been struggling like this for several moments. Don was in no way fit, and he was in no way athletic, but he had Garrity at an awkward angle. He'd been holding him off— digging his feet into the balcony floor, the soles of his shoes scuffling on the thin layer of concrete—but he knew he wouldn't be able to maintain for much longer. Garrity's muscles felt hard and taut, and Don could feel the tide turning.

In fact, he felt gravity. Every few moments, his torso struck the metal handrail, which cracked into his ribs, and his body would teeter over the edge for a half-second before he willed his momentum back toward the building.

Then he realized.

Garrity was *trying* to throw Don over the edge, even though Don was clinging with all his strength. Garrity wasn't just out to murder innocents; he'd gone full kamikaze.

He was going to hurl them *both* off the balcony.

The sneering look on Garrity's face was confirmation. The slash of a mouth with bared teeth. Eyebrows in a V. A deadly, deranged look in his eyes, which met Don's every few seconds, as though taunting him, daring him.

Don inhaled and gave a strong thrust of the arms, focusing all of his energy toward Garrity's wrist. The gun dropped and hit the floor with a heavy thud.

Don nearly smiled.

He'd gotten the gun away. He'd averted the disaster that the Carver had intended.

Once more, a sense of stunned awe swept over him.

But he was quickly brought back to the moment, as he took another half plunge over the handrail. He felt the pull of the ground below. People screamed.

This time, he wasn't able to right himself, to get his momentum going back to the building. He and Garrity were dangling over the edge. Garrity howled with delight.

More screams from below.

Don knew there was only one way to get through this.

Back in his high-roller days, he'd fancied that he knew a thing or two about real-world physics. It was as though he could will the dice to land in his favor, measuring the angle and force with which he tossed them.

He needed those real-world physics skills once more.

Because his energy was depleted. And Garrity's brute strength was nowhere near depleted.

With one final, violent tug, Garrity pulled them over the handrail.

And they both tumbled over the edge.

Don felt the ground rush up to meet him, his stomach lurching as he fell. He screamed in terror, his eyes wide and his arms flailing. Wind rushed over his face, and the sickening inevitability of the ground drew closer and closer.

He reminded himself that it was only a two-story drop. Survivable, especially if he played his cards right.

But a two-story drop didn't allow much time. His real-world physics application needed to be rapid.

He grabbed Garrity's shoulders, spun himself around the other man, saw his violent sneer of a mouth, those dark eyes...

BAM!

...and watched those eyes close instantly, blood spurting from behind.

A thunder of pain rolled through Don's arm. He looked. The hand was twisted back at an odd angle. And it wouldn't move. Broken arm.

But below him, the Carver was *entirely* broken.

And dead.

Real-world physics had come through in the end.

Groaning, Don rolled off the body.

The gasping crowd cautiously closed in around him. A man and a woman ran over, asking if he needed help, saying they were doctors.

Sirens sounded in the distance.

And Don lay on his back, looking through the neon lights and into the dark sky above.

CHAPTER FORTY-ONE

COLD CONCRETE PRESSED against the side of Silence's body, head to toe. He noticed it especially on his cheek, flat to the floor.

Wet concrete. Cold against his cheek. Going warm with blood.

Cerise, kneeling.

"My God!" she screamed. "Oh my God!"

There was no blood under Silence's cheek this time, but there was some in his mouth. He tasted it. That'll happen when you get struck in the face with a piece of rebar.

Yes, that's what had happened.

It all came back to him. Dalton had swung an eighteen-inch length of rebar, attacking from a cutout in the concrete floor.

Silence's reflexes were expertly honed, but he'd been caught off guard. He'd managed to twist away from the attack, just in time, avoiding most of the metal rod's brunt.

But not all of it.

It had grazed the edge of his chin, spinning his entire body, flashing a pulse of white over his vision, and sending him to the floor.

Culverson's ugly pig face, sneering as he swung the bat.

No, not Culverson. Dalton.

Dalton...

The man was right behind him.

Silence's fingers squeezed instinctively. But the Beretta wasn't there. He squinted.

There.

It was just a faint outline in the dusty shadows on the other side of the space.

He heard movement from behind.

Hurry.

He planted his hands on the concrete. Pushed. His head spun, heart pounded, vision blurred. He tried to focus, but the world around him was a haze of shadows and neon lights.

Fingers on his shoulder. They gave a violent shove, and his face fell back to the concrete.

Blood on the concrete.

Cerise's hand on his shoulder, dappled with rain, fingers twisted in the wet cloth of his jacket.

"Oh my God!"

Groaning, he rolled over. There was Dalton. Standing over him. Clenching the rebar, whose length stretched beneath Dalton's palm—a reverse grip.

He would plunge the bar into Silence at any moment.

And he would enjoy it. The wicked grin on his face said so.

Sometimes that's all it takes to sober a man up—the threat of imminent death.

Silence shook his head—*Cerise standing in front of him, in a T-shirt, "Why does it have to be this way?"*—and with a surge of energy, he bolted to his feet.

In the second it took to right himself, Silence saw stunned reverence blast away the stupid smile that had been on Dalton's face.

For another fraction of a second, Dalton remained stunned, then he swung the rebar.

A pointless gesture.

Silence brought the arm to a dead stop, mid-swing, catching him by the forearm. He yanked...

Snap!

...and dislocated Dalton's elbow.

Dalton howled, a sort of primordial roar that pinched his eyes shut, sent his mouth splaying wide open.

Silence sent a solid uppercut to the man's stomach, folding him, dropping him to the floor.

This man was no adversary. His stomach had been down-pillow-soft when Silence's fist connected. Dalton was fake. As fake as the characters in his scripts. Fake words. Fake bravado. As fake as any other bully.

Silence's attention flashed to Kendall's unconscious form. Breathing. Nothing more.

Silence knew his gun's location, where it had settled after it flew from his hand. It was against the opposite wall.

But he wasn't going to need it.

Not for this soft, fake, self-indulgent, cruel bully.

Dalton looked up, blinking, crying.

And Silence dropped a heavy fist into his eye.

Crack!

Blood spurted out of a gash on Dalton's cheek. He reached up, pleading.

Cerise reached, fingers spread wide, running toward him.

Cerise in a T-shirt.

Culverson's pig face. The bat.

Crack!

Silence planted another fist into Dalton's face. This one put him out.

Shit! Only two blows, and the guy was unconscious. Silence had wanted him to *feel it.*

Love? C.C. said.

Silence was panting. His fist was raised over his head, quivering.

Yes?

It's over.

But—

It's over.

Silence had wanted to do more, the demolish Dalton, this bully who'd brought so much pain.

His eyes went to Kendall again.

And he exhaled, took a few deep breaths to calm his fury.

C.C. was right. Silence had let rage take over. Even righteous assassins can suffer spiritual blowback, and it would have been a mistake indeed to continue to pulverize an unconscious man he intended to kill.

So Silence simply reached out, took hold of Dalton's head with both hands, and snapped his neck.

Silence had noticed a squarish bulge in Dalton's pocket. He reached inside, pulled out a microcassette player. After he rewound the tape for a few moments, he pressed *PLAY*.

There was the background chatter of a large crowd and the ringing sounds of slot machines. Then a man's voice, panicked.

What do you mean, Boyd?

It was Dalton.

Another man answered. He sounded older.

I mean you're done with our operation. You distributed the poisoned heroin for us, but your ineptitude has shown that you're no leader. Now that—

Silence fast-forwarded for a bit, pressed *PLAY*.

Dalton's voice again, still panicked.

I ... but... But you're from Reno.

The same older man replied.

That's what we told you. I'm from Phoenix. My friend here is from Oregon, and my other friend is from El Paso.

Silence stopped the tape, put the player in his pocket, and pondered the name.

Boyd.

The older man. And two associates from Oregon and Texas. The drugs had been poisoned, and they were the ones who did it.

Silence knew of a Boyd in the Phoenix area. One who fit the bill. He would get this intel to Watchers Specialists and have a confirmation of his suspicions within minutes.

He stood and took a moment to absorb the scene. Through an open window in the back, he saw a line of brightly colored hot air balloons in the distance, all at ground level, their inner glows pulsing in a brilliant display. Beside Silence was Dalton's body, lifeless. Farther away, Kendall's unconscious body. The empty plane of dusty concrete between the two bodies pulsed with the lights of the city.

Silence went to the other side of the space and retrieved his Beretta, placed it in his shoulder holster. Then he went to Kendall. He gently hooked one arm beneath her, hoisted her over his shoulder, and started for the stairwell.

CHAPTER FORTY-TWO

IT WAS NEARLY MIDNIGHT, and Toscani was still in his office. He had just turned off the television that Arturo had wheeled in on the cart hours earlier, and now he was tinkering on his computer, using the Internet—a specific component of the Internet that some of his younger employees referred to as the World Wide Web.

The late news had just wrapped, and while Toscani had stayed glued to the coverage all evening, he wanted even more. He'd heard that news was available around-the-clock on the Internet.

If he could just figure out how to use it.

Arturo stood behind him, and Toscani could feel the younger man's fretful energy, surely wanting to offer a simple pointer that would clarify everything, but also not wanting to insult his prideful employer.

Finally, with a grunt, Toscani tossed the mouse to the side and wheeled his chair away from the computer, leaning back. The chair squeaked.

He hooked a thumb at the computer.

"They say these things are the wave of the future," he said. "Can you believe that shit?"

Arturo scoffed in agreement, but it was pure sycophancy. Toscani knew that Arturo was an avid tech guy.

Toscani sighed. He supposed he should give his brain a break from the news, anyway. But so many tantalizing things had happened in one day. The Carver had attempted to murder people outside the charity event at the Starlight Chalice, only to be stopped by Donnie Judkins, of all people. The pair had fallen from a balcony in their struggle, and the Carver had died. Reports indicated that Judkins suffered a broken arm, but was otherwise unharmed.

Then there was Ian Dalton, this mystery man who Toscani had never met but had apparently been the cause of the killer drugs that had threatened Toscani's operation. He'd been found dead, too, in the unfinished tower right next-door to the Starlight Chalice.

And, of course, there was the balloon glow.

With so much going on, it was no wonder that Toscani couldn't make himself unplug from the news.

So much had happened in one night that he wondered as to the connection. Toscani wasn't a believer in coincidences. The Carver and the poisoned drugs had been dual threats for some time, but they both met dramatic ends in one evening. Could that be a fluke?

Or could it be Max?

Yes, there was Max, that shadowy, mysterious man who had come into Toscani's office earlier in the day with Donnie Judkins, the man who ultimately beat the Carver.

Max... who was able to easily best two of Toscani's elite guards, including Arturo.

Max... who offered only a single-syllable name—no surname, no position, no employer.

Toscani was one of the top criminal leaders in the country.

As such, he was privy to rumors that the average person wasn't.

And he'd heard rumors of a group of individuals working in secrecy within the U.S. government to correct injustices, to dole out punishments to those who escaped procedural justice. If the rumors were to be believed, this group typically rebalanced karma through assassinations.

But some rumors said that they also occasionally fixed errors by other means—getting people into prison who needed to be there. They didn't *always* kill.

Max seemed like he could be a member of just such an organization.

The computer screen behind Toscani flashed. He turned.

The entire screen had gone white.

Toscani wheeled the chair back over and grabbed the mouse he had just thrown. Clicked. The computer didn't respond to the input.

"What the hell?"

A letter appeared on the left side of the screen: *I*.

For a moment, the *I* was alone. Then a *T* followed it. Then a slew of letters fell into place until a message formed.

IT WAS A PLEASURE MEETING YOU. HAVE A NICE LIFE.
-MAX

A moment after the last letter, *X*, appeared, the entire message disappeared.

Then a plethora of documents flashed across the screen. One by one. Each of them only receiving a half second of screen time.

Invoices.

Emails.

Death threats.

Photographs.

All of it related to Toscani's empire.

Arturo had stepped up behind him, and in his deep voice he grumbled, "Holy shit."

Toscani's lips were dry. He licked them. "What does this—"

Whack!

The door swung open and cracked into the wall.

"Federal agents! Hands in the air!"

Four people burst into Toscani's office. Three men and a woman. All waving guns. All with jackets bearing the letters: *DEA*.

"Oh..." Toscani said.

Toscani admired cunning, cleverness, a perfectly-timed move.

"Touché, Max."

A smile formed, and from it, a little chuckle.

The DEA agents spread out into the room. Screaming. A pair of them rushed Arturo. The other two went for Toscani.

He raised his hands, stood up. And laughed louder.

CHAPTER FORTY-THREE

THE NEXT MORNING.

Wallace Boyd reclined on the patio of his sprawling Phoenix estate, a glass of whiskey in one hand and a cigar in the other. He looked out across the grounds, taking in the beauty of his home.

The pool with its gurgling water feature in the back. The matching hot tub. The guest house. The immaculate desert landscaping, including several prized saguaros.

It was a sign of success, and he was proud of it, but he was enjoying it with a sense of finality.

Because the partners were dead.

Boyd had gotten word twice that day.

First, around ten in the morning, he'd gotten a phone call. Greene had been found in his Lexus in the subterranean parking structure of the hotel/casino they'd stayed at in Reno. All three of the partners had agreed they were going to get the hell out of town last night, and Greene had been impatient to wait for valet parking to retrieve his car.

Someone had waited for him in the back seat and garroted him with a length of extension cord. Evidently, when hotel staff found the body that morning, the Lexus had reeked. Greene had shit himself.

An hour and a half later, another call, and Boyd learned what happened to his other partner. Like Greene, Smith hadn't made it out of Reno. Like Greene, the hotel staff had discovered Smith's body. He'd been at the desk in the corner of his suite, two bullet holes in his forehead.

Boyd had made it out of Reno last night. But he didn't feel safe. In fact, after the conversation he'd had just before his flight, he'd resigned himself to the idea that he would soon die.

Before leaving Reno, he'd called Demetrio Toscani. He'd told the old Italian of the plot that had been hatched against him. He'd done so in a no-harm-no-foul sort of way, like shaking hands after the game, congratulating the team you beat. Reciprocally, Toscani had said he respected Boyd's tenacity, and he offered him a bit of advice.

No, not advice.

It had been a warning.

He'd told him of a rumored group of individuals working in secret within the government, people who sent out their own unsanctioned assassins to right wrongs.

Boyd had thanked Toscani, but he hadn't worried much about the man's warning, even after he woke up to the news that Toscani had been arrested by the DEA shortly after Boyd had gotten on the red-eye out of Reno. Besides, the group Toscani mentioned supposedly used assassins, not federal warrants.

It wasn't until Boyd received the phone call regarding Greene that he began to worry. When he got the second call, about Smith, he knew he was going to die.

So for the last several hours, Boyd had enjoyed booze and cigars and saguaros and that wonderful dry air he loved so much. Simple comforts on the way out.

There was a sound from behind.

Boyd sighed, puffed his cigar, and didn't turn, even when the figure stepped up beside him. From his peripheral, Boyd saw a large man with sharp features in dark dress-casual clothes. A suppressed pistol hung long at his side.

He sat in the chair beside Boyd, stared at him.

Boyd turned.

The man was lengthy. White. Maybe middle-aged. Brown eyes. Dark hair, falling in choppy strands over his high cheek-bones. Silk V-neck shirt. Bead bracelets poked out of the cuff of his sport coat.

Boyd offered a gracious bow of the head. "What is it, about a two-hour flight between here and Reno?"

The man nodded.

Boyd took another puff of his cigar, looked off into the desert. "You didn't kill Toscani. Lots of people deal drugs."

"Not a lot of people..." the man said and swallowed. "Deal poison."

Boyd froze, then slowly rotated to look at the other man. The voice had been hideous. If he was using it as a scare tactic, it certainly did the trick. Truly unnerving.

A cordless phone rested on a metal side table between them. Boyd nodded toward it.

"May I call my granddaughter first?" Boyd said. "Hear her voice one last time? It would mean the—"

The man raised his pistol and shot Boyd in the face.

CHAPTER FORTY-FOUR

DON UNLOCKED THE DOOR. But didn't open it. He groaned.

Room 134. The Morrice Motel. Another crappy place. Another pay-by-cash, can-you-keep-a-secret?, tell-no-one-I'm-here situation.

Nothing had changed.

The Morrice was in Lockwood, a tiny place on the Truckee River, within the Reno metro area but a few miles outside the city. Lockwood was just fine—idyllic, even—but the Morrice Motel was not.

Yep, some things never change. Some luck never changes.

Snake eyes, again and again.

He held a plastic sack of "groceries" he'd gotten from the convenience store at an I-80 truck stop on the other side of the river. His other arm was in a sling. The pain meds were numbing his body, but they were doing nothing for his mood.

He pushed the door open and immediately saw a figure in the room, shrouded in darkness, just a silhouette at the tiny table in the back.

Don's heart didn't jump. He didn't even break stride. He just proceeded into the room.

"Hi Max," he said.

The silhouette grunted a return salutation.

Sam flipped on the lights, revealing a wood-paneled, well-worn interior, a freak-show bed, and Max.

Max stared at him, blank-faced.

Don stepped past the big guy, going to the bathroom counter, underneath which was a miniature refrigerator. He retrieved the microwavable meal from the plastic sack and placed it on the refrigerator's top shelf. The tiny freezer on top wouldn't accommodate his four-ounce cup of Ben & Jerry's, however.

So, screw it.

He retrieved the plastic spoon he'd gotten at the gas station, took the lid off the Cherry Garcia, propped the carton on top of his sling, and took a bite as he turned to face Max.

"You found me a lot quicker this time," he said.

Max shrugged.

"You didn't make it..." he said and swallowed. "As difficult."

Don took another bite. "Maybe I wanted to be found. I don't know."

Max looked as stony and stoic as ever, but he also looked exhausted. If last night's adventures had taken this bad of a toll on Don, he could only imagine what hell Max had gone through.

"Reno's going to give me the key to the city. Did you hear that?"

Max nodded.

"The man who took out the Carver," Don said and laughed. His eyes immediately roamed the shitty motel room. "A key to the city, but I'm still on the run. Creditors don't much care for civic heroes." He sighed. "How is—"

"Kendall's fine," Max said and swallowed. "So is Cooper."

Don smiled. "Good."

He lifted another bite of ice cream. Stopped. The spoon hung halfway to his mouth. He looked at the plastic utensil, the matted carpet below it, then put the spoon back in the cup and placed the cup on the counter.

He rested his ass against the counter, squared up to the other man. "I'm tired of running, Max."

"I know," Max said and swallowed. "You don't have to anymore."

"I just told you that—"

"My organization..." Max said and swallowed. "Paid your debts."

It was a good thing Don was leaning against the sink, because otherwise the wave of lightheadedness might have toppled him over.

"*What?*"

Max just nodded.

"But, how?"

"Don't worry about it." He swallowed. "Just go back to Reno..." Another swallow. "And live your life."

He lifted his big frame out of the chair, nodded as he passed, and left.

CHAPTER FORTY-FIVE

SILENCE STOOD beside the Dodge Spirit, waiting. The sun was slowly setting over the mountains in the distance, and the sunset was just as magnificent as the previous day's, only more purple this time, less orange. The air had gone a bit chilly, and Silence crossed his arms over his chest, pulling his sport coat in tighter.

The Spirit was a rental. It had Wyoming plates. Cerise would be returning it at the airport drop-off momentarily.

He stared across the parking lot, full of vehicles, at the casino/resort tower beyond, the one where Cerise had been staying. The tower cast a long shadow in the dying sunlight, as did the vehicles and lamp poles.

Silence had returned from Arizona an hour earlier, before his stop at Lockwood. He'd made it back to Reno proper just in time. Cerise told him on the phone that she'd spent the day in bed, nothing but room service and television, recovering from the previous day's events. She'd maintained that she was a cryptographer, not an assassin like him, and for her, recuperation was a requisite after all that had happened. He agreed.

As for Silence, he'd not only touched base with Judkins—and Wallace Boyd—but he'd also spent the in-between moments processing a memory that had resurfaced.

Doc Hazel had told him that some of the memories might break through.

She was correct.

———

It had been two and a half years ago.

The memory was preceded by nothing—empty, dark haze. Silence had no idea how he'd gotten to that suite, why he was there, or why Cerise was knocking on his door, but the next few moments returned fully formed, crystal-clear, entirely intact.

Tapping at his door. Relentless. Rapid. Loud.

Tap-tap-tap-tap-tap.

Silence growled and rushed across the suite. It was in downtown Spokane. A sprawling unit with two bedrooms and two full baths. All blacks and grays and stainless steels, perfectly fitting Silence's aesthetic.

The lights were off, and the only glow came from the open door to the bedroom in the back. He'd been prepared to climb into bed when the tapping started.

Tap-tap-tap-tap-tap.

As he thundered to the foyer, he realized he was shirtless. He should cover up.

Tap-tap-tap-tap-tap.

Screw it.

When he threw open the door, he found Cerise dressed in an entirely opposite manner.

A long T-shirt.

And nothing more.

He could tell she wasn't even wearing a bra.

Her eyes were wet with tears. One escaped, raced down her cheek. Her lips were wet too, trembling.

"Let me in!" she said.

"No."

"Let. Me. *In!*"

Silence scowled at her, fuming. But she was being loud in the hallway, and Silence didn't want trouble with the neighbors. While chasing down someone as ruthless as Culverson, the last thing he needed was to get sidetracked by his hotel's management.

He stepped aside. Cerise rushed past him.

He closed the door and faced her. She'd stopped in the middle of the foyer, a dark figure, hardly lit. Bare feet on the polished black flooring. A T-shirt and nothing more. Wet cheeks, glistening in the dim light.

He stayed rooted right where he was, only a couple of feet past the door. Cerise approached.

"Why not?" she said.

"You know why."

"Because you're engaged." She looked at him, lip trembling harder, building her conviction. "Know what I think? I think you're not really engaged. I think that's a lie."

Silence's entire frame tautened.

"That's a *hell* of an assumption," he growled.

"Oh? Then tell me I'm wrong!"

Silence didn't respond. He looked away from her eyes.

Cerise was a cryptographer. She decoded things for a living. She'd decoded him.

She stepped even closer, only inches away. She put her hand on his shoulder.

He glanced over. Saw her hand. Her fingers rested on his bare flesh.

"Why does it have to be this way?" she said.

Silence didn't respond.

"Please..."

"No."

Cerise shuddered. "Then ... then give me a kiss, at least. You know what I've been through, why your organization reached out to me. Give me that. Just a kiss."

"No."

But Cerise's eyes were already fluttering closed, coming toward him as she lifted onto her toes.

She drew closer.

Closer.

Her lips met his. Moving. He did not kiss her back.

She lowered back down and looked to the floor.

"I'll see you tomorrow," she said.

She drifted past him and let herself out. When the door shut, Silence turned back around, locked it, then retreated for the light flowing out of the bedroom door.

And remembered he hadn't washed his face yet.

The memory faded away with thoughts not of Cerise, but of a washcloth.

———

Silence had been seeing the memory all day long.

Typically, his overactive mind would spend way too much time analyzing something, replaying a notion repeatedly. This time, though, the newly acquired memory just sat there. Like a presence. He didn't dissect it. He didn't ruminate. He just let it be. Exactly like C.C. would have told him to do.

Ahead, Cerise crossed through the parking lot, dragging a piece of wheeled luggage. She wore jeans and a sweatshirt—ready for a long flight back to D.C. Her figure and the luggage cast long shadows that joined the rest of those slashing through the expansive lot.

She stopped a few feet away from him, resting the luggage upright. They regarded each other.

"A proper goodbye this time," she said with a smile before reading something in his face. "You don't remember our last goodbye, do you?"

Silence shook his head. "No, ma'am."

"Ma'am?"

"They told me the news," Silence said and swallowed. "That they recruited you." Another swallow. "Congrats."

That morning, the Watchers had informed Silence they'd reached out to Cerise the previous evening. With her upstanding character, tenacious attitude, esoteric skill set, and in light of the events in both Spokane and Reno, they'd offered Cerise a position in the organization.

She'd accepted.

Specialists like Cerise were the lifeblood of the Watchers, providing all the organization's logistical and technical needs. Specialists were also higher up the ladder than Assets like Silence.

Hence the "ma'am."

Cerise waved it off.

"Oh, fiddle-faddle," she said, using another one of her old-fashioned words. "They already told me we'll never work together. Conflict of interests. So let's keep it personal for these last few moments together, all right?"

Silence nodded.

There was another moment as they regarded each other. Cerise's fingers fidgeted on the handle of her luggage.

"Thank you," she said. "Not for this. For Spokane. You don't remember, but you truly helped."

Silence was stubborn and pragmatic, so it seemed wrong to offer a "you're welcome" for something he couldn't be sure had even happened.

Regardless, it felt like the right thing to do. So he did it.

"You're welcome."

Cerise's eyes went to the Dodge, back to Silence.

"I'd better go. I won't ask for a kiss this time. I remember how that turned out." She snickered, almost defeated. "But how about a handshake?"

She stuck out her hand.

"I'll do you one better," Silence said and swallowed. "How about a hug?"

He opened his arms wide.

Cerise smiled.

"Deal."

She stepped forward.

And they embraced.

ALSO BY ERIK CARTER

Novella

Get Down

ACKNOWLEDGMENTS

For their involvement with *Quiet as the Grave*, I would like to give a sincere thank you to:

My ARC readers, for providing reviews and catching typos. Thanks!

Printed in Great Britain
by Amazon